NO FEAR

The Canterbury Tales
The Scarlet Letter

SHAKESPEARE

As You Like It
The Comedy of Errors
Hamlet
Henry IV, Parts One and Two
Henry V
Julius Caesar
King Lear
Macbeth
The Merchant of Venice
A Midsummer Night's Dream
Much Ado About Nothing
Othello
Richard III
Romeo and Juliet
Sonnets
The Taming of the Shrew
The Tempest
Twelfth Night

NO FEAR

BEOWULF

© 2017 by Sterling Publishing Co., Inc.

SPARKNOTES is a registered trademark of SparkNotes LLC

Spark Publishing
A Division of Barnes & Noble
1166 Avenue of the Americas
New York, NY 10036
www.sparknotes.com

ISBN-13: 978-1-4549-2521-7

Please submit changes or report errors to www.sparknotes.com/errors.

Printed in the United States

FEAR NOT.

Have you ever tried to read *Beowulf* and realized midway through the second sentence that you were already lost? *No Fear: Beowulf* will change all that. You won't have to worry about losing the thread anymore. Whenever the poem's language becomes too convoluted to follow, simply turn to the end of the chapter for a prose explanation that's easy to understand. Soon you'll be reading *Beowulf* fearlessly—and actually enjoying it.

No Fear: Beowulf puts a modern spin on the classic poem, using the kind of English people actually speak today. When *Beowulf* makes your head spin, our translation will help you sort out what's happening, who's saying what, and why.

Contents

Characters

Beowulf—The protagonist of the poem. Beowulf is a Geatish hero who fights the monster Grendel, Grendel's mother, and a fire-breathing dragon. Beowulf's exploits prove him to be the strongest, ablest warrior of his time. In his youth, he personifies the values of the heroic culture. In his old age, he proves a wise and effective ruler.

Grendel—A demon descended from Cain. Grendel preys on Hrothgar's warriors in the king's mead-hall, Heorot. Because Grendel's ruthless and miserable existence is part of the retribution exacted by God for Cain's murder of Abel, Grendel fits solidly within the ethos of vengeance that governs the world of the poem.

Grendel's Mother—A demon even more monstrous than Grendel. Grendel's mother seeks revenge on Hrothgar's men for the death of her son. Beowulf journeys to her magical, creature-filled lair beneath the swamp in order to defeat her.

King Hrothgar—The king of the Danes. Hrothgar enjoys military success and prosperity until Grendel comes to terrorize his realm. Hrothgar is a wise and aged ruler, and he represents a different kind of leadership from that exhibited by the youthful warrior Beowulf. He is a father figure to Beowulf and a model for the kind of king that Beowulf becomes.

Unferth—A Danish warrior who is jealous of Beowulf. Unferth is unable or unwilling to fight Grendel, thus proving himself inferior to Beowulf.

Hygelac—Beowulf's uncle, king of the Geats, and husband of Hygd. Hygelac heartily welcomes Beowulf upon his return from Denmark.

Ecgtheow—Beowulf's father, Hygelac's brother-in-law, and Hrothgar's friend. Ecgtheow is dead by the time the story begins, but he lives on through the noble reputation that he made for himself and in his dutiful son's remembrances.

King Hrethel—The Geatish king who took Beowulf in as a ward after the death of Ecgtheow, Beowulf's father.

The dragon—An ancient, powerful serpent that guards a hoard of treasure. Beowulf fights the dragon in the third and final part of the epic.

Wiglaf—A young kinsman and retainer of Beowulf. Wiglaf helps Beowulf in the fight against the dragon after the other warriors run away. Wiglaf adheres to the heroic code, thereby proving himself a suitable successor to Beowulf.

NO FEAR

BEOWULF

*sparknotes

Prelude of the Founder
of the Danish House

Lo, praise of the prowess of people-kings
of spear-armed Danes, in days long sped,
we have heard, and what honor the athelings won!
Oft Scyld the Scefing from squadroned foes,
from many a tribe, the mead-bench tore,
awing the earls. Since erst he lay
friendless, a foundling, fate repaid him:
for he waxed under welkin, in wealth he throve,
till before him the folk, both far and near,
who house by the whale-path, heard his mandate,
gave him gifts: a good king he!
To him an heir was afterward born,
a son in his halls, whom heaven sent
to favor the folk, feeling their woe
that erst they had lacked an earl for leader
so long a while; the Lord endowed him,
the Wielder of Wonder, with world's renown.
Famed was this Beowulf: far flew the boast of him,
son of Scyld, in the Scandian lands.
So becomes it a youth to quit him well
with his father's friends, by fee and gift,
that to aid him, aged, in after days,
come warriors willing, should war draw nigh,
liegemen loyal: by lauded deeds
shall an earl have honor in every clan.

Forth he fared at the fated moment,
sturdy Scyld to the shelter of God.
Then they bore him over to ocean's billow,
loving clansmen, as late he charged them,
while wielded words the winsome Scyld,

the leader beloved who long had ruled....
In the roadstead rocked a ring-dight vessel,
ice-flecked, outbound, atheling's barge:
there laid they down their darling lord
on the breast of the boat, the breaker-of-rings,
by the mast the mighty one. Many a treasure
fetched from far was freighted with him.
No ship have I known so nobly dight
with weapons of war and weeds of battle,
with breastplate and blade: on his bosom lay
a heaped hoard that hence should go
far o'er the flood with him floating away.
No less these loaded the lordly gifts,
thanes' huge treasure, than those had done
who in former time forth had sent him
sole on the seas, a suckling child.
High o'er his head they hoist the standard,
a gold-wove banner; let billows take him,
gave him to ocean. Grave were their spirits,
mournful their mood. No man is able
to say in sooth, no son of the halls,
no hero 'neath heaven,—who harbored that freight!

Prelude of the Founder of the Danish House

LONG ago, the Spear-Danes and their kings were a mighty people. We have all heard about their power and glory. We have heard of Scyld Scefing, who destroyed his enemies and their drinking halls. Though he was an orphan, he rose to become king, and his people showered him with gifts. He was a great king. The Lord of all life knew how much the people had suffered without a leader, so he sent the king a gift from heaven, a son called Beow. This boy, who lived before our Beowulf, was famous throughout the northern lands, and he behaved well in his youth, handing out gifts and earning the friendship and favor of many men that he would have to call on later in battle. In any kingdom, actions like this are a sure path to greatness and power.

Scyld died in the prime of life. He had ordered his men to send his body out to sea. They put their beloved king in his boat and filled it with more treasure, swords, and armor than I've ever seen. They covered him with the treasure, which was sent to sea with his body. He was sent upon the sea just like he had been sent upon the sea of life in his youth. There was a gold banner flying from the mast of the ship, and it flapped with the breeze that carried him away. He and his treasure sailed into the unknown. His people mourned deeply.

Chapter 1

Now Beowulf bode in the burg of the Scyldings,
leader beloved, and long he ruled
in fame with all folk, since his father had gone
away from the world, till awoke an heir,
haughty Healfdene, who held through life,
sage and sturdy, the Scyldings glad.
Then, one after one, there woke to him,
to the chieftain of clansmen, children four:
Heorogar, then Hrothgar, then Halga brave;
and I heard that—was—'s queen,
the Heathoscylfing's helpmate dear.
To Hrothgar was given such glory of war,
such honor of combat, that all his kin
obeyed him gladly till great grew his band
of youthful comrades. It came in his mind
to bid his henchmen a hall uprear,
a master mead-house, mightier far
than ever was seen by the sons of earth,
and within it, then, to old and young
he would all allot that the Lord had sent him,
save only the land and the lives of his men.
Wide, I heard, was the work commanded,
for many a tribe this mid-earth round,
to fashion the folkstead. It fell, as he ordered,
in rapid achievement that ready it stood there,
of halls the noblest: Heorot he named it
whose message had might in many a land.
Not reckless of promise, the rings he dealt,
treasure at banquet: there towered the hall,
high, gabled wide, the hot surge waiting
of furious flame. Nor far was that day
when father and son-in-law stood in feud

for warfare and hatred that woke again.
With envy and anger an evil spirit
endured the dole in his dark abode,
that he heard each day the din of revel
high in the hall: there harps rang out,
clear song of the singer. He sang who knew
tales of the early time of man,
how the Almighty made the earth,
fairest fields enfolded by water,
set, triumphant, sun and moon
for a light to lighten the land-dwellers,
and braided bright the breast of earth
with limbs and leaves, made life for all
of mortal beings that breathe and move.

So lived the clansmen in cheer and revel
a winsome life, till one began
to fashion evils, that field of hell.
Grendel this monster grim was called,
march-riever mighty, in moorland living,
in fen and fastness; fief of the giants
the hapless wight a while had kept
since the Creator his exile doomed.
On kin of Cain was the killing avenged
by sovran God for slaughtered Abel.
Ill fared his feud, and far was he driven,
for the slaughter's sake, from sight of men.
Of Cain awoke all that woful breed,
Etins and elves and evil-spirits,
as well as the giants that warred with God
weary while: but their wage was paid them!

Chapter 1

BEOWULF became the ruler of the Spear-Danes and was beloved by all. He had an heir, the great Halfdane, whose wisdom and sturdiness guided and protected the people. Halfdane had three sons—Heorogar, Hrothgar, and Halga—and a daughter, who married Onela and became queen of the Swedes. Hrothgar was such a great warrior that men were eager to fight alongside him. His army grew large. He decided to build an enormous hall, the largest anyone had ever seen. From there, he would rule and give everything he could to his people, except for land and his men's lives. He brought in workmen from all over the world, and his immense and noble hall was soon completed. He named it Heorot. Once inside, he kept his promise to give gifts and treasure to his people. But outside the towering walls of Heorot, death and destruction waited. The day was coming when hatred and murder would return to tear men apart. A demon stalked outside, and he could hardly stand the sounds of music and singing that came from Heorot. The Spear-Danes sang about the origin of the world and the glory of the Almighty, who made them and everything they saw.

The people lived in happiness until the demon began his evil work. The demon was named Grendel. He lived in the swamps nearby. His Creator had banished him to live among the monsters of Cain's family. God had driven Cain out of the company of men after he murdered his brother Abel. From Cain sprang a race of giants and elves and evil spirits. They fought against God, though they had no chance of winning.

Chapter 2

WENT he forth to find at fall of night
that haughty house, and heed wherever
the Ring-Danes, outrevelled, to rest had gone.
Found within it the atheling band
asleep after feasting and fearless of sorrow,
of human hardship. Unhallowed wight,
grim and greedy, he grasped betimes,
wrathful, reckless, from resting-places,
thirty of the thanes, and thence he rushed
fain of his fell spoil, faring homeward,
laden with slaughter, his lair to seek.
Then at the dawning, as day was breaking,
the might of Grendel to men was known;
then after wassail was wail uplifted,
loud moan in the morn. The mighty chief,
atheling excellent, unblithe sat,
labored in woe for the loss of his thanes,
when once had been traced the trail of the fiend,
spirit accurst: too cruel that sorrow,
too long, too loathsome. Not late the respite;
with night returning, anew began
ruthless murder; he recked no whit,
firm in his guilt, of the feud and crime.
They were easy to find who elsewhere sought
in room remote their rest at night,
bed in the bowers, when that bale was shown,
was seen in sooth, with surest token,—
the hall-thane's hate. Such held themselves
far and fast who the fiend outran!
Thus ruled unrighteous and raged his fill
one against all; until empty stood
that lordly building, and long it bode so.

ORIGINAL TEXT

***

Twelve years' tide the trouble he bore,
sovran of Scyldings, sorrows in plenty,
boundless cares. There came unhidden
tidings true to the tribes of men,
in sorrowful songs, how ceaselessly Grendel
harassed Hrothgar, what hate he bore him,
what murder and massacre, many a year,
feud unfading,—refused consent
to deal with any of Daneland's earls,
make pact of peace, or compound for gold:
still less did the wise men ween to get
great fee for the feud from his fiendish hands.
But the evil one ambushed old and young
death-shadow dark, and dogged them still,
lured, or lurked in the livelong night
of misty moorlands: men may say not
where the haunts of these Hell-Runes be.
Such heaping of horrors the hater of men,
lonely roamer, wrought unceasing,
harassings heavy. O'er Heorot he lorded,
gold-bright hall, in gloomy nights;
and ne'er could the prince approach his throne,
—'twas judgment of God,—or have joy in his hall.
Sore was the sorrow to Scyldings'-friend,
heart-rending misery. Many nobles
sat assembled, and searched out counsel
how it were best for bold-hearted men
against harassing terror to try their hand.
Whiles they vowed in their heathen fanes
altar-offerings, asked with words
that the slayer-of-souls would succor give them
for the pain of their people. Their practice this,
their heathen hope; 'twas Hell they thought of

in mood of their mind. Almighty they knew not,
Doomsman of Deeds and dreadful Lord,
nor Heaven's-Helmet heeded they ever,
Wielder-of-Wonder.—Woe for that man
who in harm and hatred hales his soul
to fiery embraces;—nor favor nor change
awaits he ever. But well for him
that after death-day may draw to his Lord,
and friendship find in the Father's arms!

Chapter 2

S o in the nighttime, Grendel went to the hall to watch the men, who had been drinking. He came upon them asleep, completely oblivious to the sorrow and pain that awaited them. Full of wrath, Grendel grabbed thirty of the men and took them back to his lair. When dawn broke, the men in the hall saw what Grendel had done. They were beside themselves with grief. Even their fearless leader sat paralyzed, completely overwhelmed by the destruction Grendel had caused. But they couldn't grieve for long, as Grendel returned the next night to claim more victims. Men could be seen fleeing the hall for safety, running to escape Grendel's hatred. The great hall soon stood empty.

For twelve years Hrothgar suffered as a result of Grendel's attacks. The whole world heard of Grendel's rage and the murders he carried out on Hrothgar's people. Grendel refused to stop, even for huge sums of gold, and no man would dare try to negotiate with the foul monster. Old and young alike were terrified, as Grendel hunted them at night in the misty swamps, never stopping his lonely war. Once night fell, he was the ruler of Heorot. Hrothgar was heartbroken. His advisors all offered ideas of how best to deal with Grendel. They even made offerings to pagan gods and asked devils to come to their aid. That was how little hope they had left. They were heathens and they did not know that they could turn to Almighty God, Lord of the Heavens. Pity the man who turns to hell for help, but well for the faithful man who can find God's welcome when he dies.

Chapter 3

THUS seethed unceasing the son of Healfdene
with the woe of these days; not wisest men
assuaged his sorrow; too sore the anguish,
loathly and long, that lay on his folk,
most baneful of burdens and bales of the night.

This heard in his home Hygelac's thane,
great among Geats, of Grendel's doings.
He was the mightiest man of valor
in that same day of this our life,
stalwart and stately. A stout wave-walker
he bade make ready. Yon battle-king, said he,
far o'er the swan-road he fain would seek,
the noble monarch who needed men!
The prince's journey by prudent folk
was little blamed, though they loved him dear;
they whetted the hero, and hailed good omens.
And now the bold one from bands of Geats
comrades chose, the keenest of warriors
e'er he could find; with fourteen men
the sea-wood he sought, and, sailor proved,
led them on to the land's confines.

Time had now flown; afloat was the ship,
boat under bluff. On board they climbed,
warriors ready; waves were churning
sea with sand; the sailors bore
on the breast of the bark their bright array,
their mail and weapons: the men pushed off,
on its willing way, the well-braced craft.
Then moved o'er the waters by might of the wind
that bark like a bird with breast of foam,

Beowulf

till in season due, on the second day,
the curved prow such course had run
that sailors now could see the land,
sea-cliffs shining, steep high hills,
headlands broad. Their haven was found,
their journey ended. Up then quickly
the Weders' clansmen climbed ashore,
anchored their sea-wood, with armor clashing
and gear of battle: God they thanked
or passing in peace o'er the paths of the sea.

Now saw from the cliff a Scylding clansman,
a warden that watched the water-side,
how they bore o'er the gangway glittering shields,
war-gear in readiness; wonder seized him
to know what manner of men they were.
Straight to the strand his steed he rode,
Hrothgar's henchman; with hand of might
he shook his spear, and spake in parley.
"Who are ye, then, ye armed men,
mailed folk, that yon mighty vessel
have urged thus over the ocean ways,
here o'er the waters? A warden I,
sentinel set o'er the sea-march here,
lest any foe to the folk of Danes
with harrying fleet should harm the land.
No aliens ever at ease thus bore them,
linden-wielders: yet word-of-leave
clearly ye lack from clansmen here,
my folk's agreement.—A greater ne'er saw I
of warriors in world than is one of you,—
yon hero in harness! No henchman he
worthied by weapons, if witness his features,
his peerless presence! I pray you, though, tell

your folk and home, lest hence ye fare
suspect to wander your way as spies
in Danish land. Now, dwellers afar,
ocean-travellers, take from me
simple advice: the sooner the better
I hear of the country whence ye came."

Chapter 3

THE wisest men could offer no real help to Hrothgar, who suffered unimaginable sorrow. His people struggled to endure the horrors of the night.

Grendel's attacks were talked about in the nearby kingdom of the Geats. Hygelac, the ruler of the Geats, had a great warrior in his command, a nobleman who was the bravest man alive. No one compared to him. When he heard of Grendel's deeds, this man ordered that his warship be made ready to sail. He announced that he would sail to the aid of Hrothgar. Though the Geats loved him greatly, they did not stop him from going. They praised him and looked for good omens that foretold success. And the brave man gathered the fourteen best warriors of the Geats and prepared to sail.

The boat was ready in the harbor. The men carried their shining weapons and armor on board, while the waves slapped the side of the ship. They pushed off and caught the wind. The boat was like a bird skimming the surface of the sea. On the second day, they saw tall cliffs ahead and knew their journey was over. They anchored their boat and leapt ashore, their weapons and armor clanging. They thanked God for a safe voyage.

Up on the cliff, one of Hrothgar's guards saw the men unloading their shields and weapons. He raced down to the shore on his horse and confronted the men, shaking his spear while he spoke, "Who are you? Why have you sailed here fully armed? You don't have permission from my people to land here with weapons out. I've never seen anything like this in all my days as a guard. And what a mighty warrior your leader is! An honest-to-goodness hero. But you better tell me where you're from and what you're doing here, unless you want people to think you are spies. The sooner you tell me, the better."

Chapter 4

To him the stateliest spake in answer;
the warriors' leader his word-hoard unlocked:—
"We are by kin of the clan of Geats,
and Hygelac's own hearth-fellows we.
To folk afar was my father known,
noble atheling, Ecgtheow named.
Full of winters, he fared away
aged from earth; he is honored still
through width of the world by wise men all.
To thy lord and liege in loyal mood
we hasten hither, to Healfdene's son,
people-protector: be pleased to advise us!
To that mighty-one come we on mickle errand,
to the lord of the Danes; nor deem I right
that aught be hidden. We hear—thou knowest
if sooth it is—the saying of men,
that amid the Scyldings a scathing monster,
dark ill-doer, in dusky nights
shows terrific his rage unmatched,
hatred and murder. To Hrothgar I
in greatness of soul would succor bring,
so the Wise-and-Brave may worst his foes,—
if ever the end of ills is fated,
of cruel contest, if cure shall follow,
and the boiling care-waves cooler grow;
else ever afterward anguish-days
he shall suffer in sorrow while stands in place
high on its hill that house unpeered!"

Astride his steed, the strand-ward answered,
clansman unquailing: "The keen-souled thane
must be skilled to sever and sunder duly

words and works, if he well intends.
I gather, this band is graciously bent
to the Scyldings' master. March, then, bearing
weapons and weeds the way I show you.
I will bid my men your boat meanwhile
to guard for fear lest foemen come,—
your new-tarred ship by shore of ocean
faithfully watching till once again
it waft o'er the waters those well-loved thanes,
—winding-neck'd wood,—to Weders' bounds,
heroes such as the hest of fate
shall succor and save from the shock of war."

They bent them to march,—the boat lay still,
fettered by cable and fast at anchor,
broad-bosomed ship.—Then shone the boars
over the cheek-guard; chased with gold,
keen and gleaming, guard it kept
o'er the man of war, as marched along
heroes in haste, till the hall they saw,
broad of gable and bright with gold:
that was the fairest, 'mid folk of earth,
of houses 'neath heaven, where Hrothgar lived,
and the gleam of it lightened o'er lands afar.
The sturdy shieldsman showed that bright
burg-of-the-boldest; bade them go
straightway thither; his steed then turned,
hardy hero, and hailed them thus:—
"Tis time that I fare from you. Father Almighty
in grace and mercy guard you well,
safe in your seekings. Seaward I go,
'gainst hostile warriors hold my watch."

Chapter 4

THE leader spoke. "We are Geats, and Hygelac is our ruler back home. My father was Ecgtheow, a noble warrior. He lived many years, and wise men still honor him. We are on our way to your lord, Halfdane's son, Hrothgar. Please help us in our errand. We have come to help the lord of the Danes. We have nothing to hide. We have heard of the evil monster that murders your people in the night. We want to help Hrothgar defeat this awful enemy and restore peace to the land and to his soul, if such a thing is possible. Otherwise he will suffer for the rest of his days while his hall sits empty."

From his horse, the guard answered, "A smart man knows the difference between words and actions. I believe you when you say that you want to help us. So get your weapons and let's go—I'll show you the way. I'll leave some guards with your boat. They'll keep it safe until it's time for you to sail back home. May fate keep you heroes safe."

They set out, leaving their ship anchored in the sea. The warriors marched quickly and soon saw the hall, enormous and shining with gold. Hrothgar's hall was the most beautiful house on earth and its glory extended to distant lands. The guard showed them to the house and then turned back, saying, "I have to go back to my post at the shore. May Almighty God protect you."

Chapter 5

STONE-BRIGHT the street: it showed the way
to the crowd of clansmen. Corselets glistened
hand-forged, hard; on their harness bright
the steel ring sang, as they strode along
in mail of battle, and marched to the hall.
There, weary of ocean, the wall along
they set their bucklers, their broad shields, down,
and bowed them to bench: the breastplates clanged,
war-gear of men; their weapons stacked,
spears of the seafarers stood together,
gray-tipped ash: that iron band
was worthily weaponed!—A warrior proud
asked of the heroes their home and kin.
"Whence, now, bear ye burnished shields,
harness gray and helmets grim,
spears in multitude? Messenger, I,
Hrothgar's herald! Heroes so many
ne'er met I as strangers of mood so strong.
'Tis plain that for prowess, not plunged into exile,
for high-hearted valor, Hrothgar ye seek!"

Him the sturdy-in-war bespake with words,
proud earl of the Weders answer made,
hardy 'neath helmet:—"Hygelac's, we,
fellows at board; I am Beowulf named.
I am seeking to say to the son of Healfdene
this mission of mine, to thy master-lord,
the doughty prince, if he deign at all
grace that we greet him, the good one, now."

Wulfgar spake, the Wendles' chieftain,
whose might of mind to many was known,

his courage and counsel: "The king of Danes,
the Scyldings' friend, I fain will tell,
the Breaker-of-Rings, as the boon thou askest,
the famed prince, of thy faring hither,
and, swiftly after, such answer bring
as the doughty monarch may deign to give."
Hied then in haste to where Hrothgar sat
white-haired and old, his earls about him,
till the stout thane stood at the shoulder there
of the Danish king: good courtier he!
Wulfgar spake to his winsome lord:—
"Hither have fared to thee far-come men
o'er the paths of ocean, people of Geatland;
and the stateliest there by his sturdy band
is Beowulf named. This boon they seek,
that they, my master, may with thee
have speech at will: nor spurn their prayer
to give them hearing, gracious Hrothgar!
In weeds of the warrior worthy they,
methinks, of our liking; their leader most surely,
a hero that hither his henchmen has led."

Chapter 5

THEY made their way up the path to the hall, their armor shining brightly. Exhausted, they put their shields down against the wall of the hall and rested on the benches. Their weapons were stacked up nearby. One of Hrothgar's warriors approached them. "Where do you come from with so much armor? I've never seen so many brave strangers before. You come to Hrothgar looking for glory, not shelter."

Their leader replied. "I am Beowulf, and we are Hygelac's men. If your master, the son of Halfdane, will meet with me, I will tell him our mission."

Wulfgar, one of the local chieftains who was famous for his courage and wisdom, responded. "I will give the king of Danes your message and will return quickly with his answer." Wulfgar hurried off to old Hrothgar, who sat surrounded by his men. "These men have come across the sea from Geatland," he said to his king, "and their leader is named Beowulf. They would like to speak with you. They seem like worthy warriors to me, especially their leader, who looks like a true hero."

Chapter 6

HROTHGAR answered, helmet of Scyldings:—
"I knew him of yore in his youthful days;
his aged father was Ecgtheow named,
to whom, at home, gave Hrethel the Geat
his only daughter. Their offspring bold
fares hither to seek the steadfast friend.
And seamen, too, have said me this,—
who carried my gifts to the Geatish court,
thither for thanks,—he has thirty men's
heft of grasp in the gripe of his hand,
the bold-in-battle. Blessed God
out of his mercy this man hath sent
to Danes of the West, as I ween indeed,
against horror of Grendel. I hope to give
the good youth gold for his gallant thought.
Be thou in haste, and bid them hither,
clan of kinsmen, to come before me;
and add this word,—they are welcome guests
to folk of the Danes."
[To the door of the hall
Wulfgar went] and the word declared:—
"To you this message my master sends,
East-Danes' king, that your kin he knows,
hardy heroes, and hails you all
welcome hither o'er waves of the sea!
Ye may wend your way in war-attire,
and under helmets Hrothgar greet;
but let here the battle-shields bide your parley,
and wooden war-shafts wait its end."

Uprose the mighty one, ringed with his men,
brave band of thanes: some bode without,

Beowulf

battle-gear guarding, as bade the chief.
Then hied that troop where the herald led them,
under Heorot's roof: [the hero strode,]
hardy 'neath helm, till the hearth he neared.
Beowulf spake,—his breastplate gleamed,
war-net woven by wit of the smith:—
"Thou Hrothgar, hail! Hygelac's I,
kinsman and follower. Fame a plenty
have I gained in youth! These Grendel-deeds
I heard in my home-land heralded clear.
Seafarers say how stands this hall,
of buildings best, for your band of thanes
empty and idle, when evening sun
in the harbor of heaven is hidden away.
So my vassals advised me well,—
brave and wise, the best of men,—
O sovran Hrothgar, to seek thee here,
for my nerve and my might they knew full well.
Themselves had seen me from slaughter come
blood-flecked from foes, where five I bound,
and that wild brood worsted. I' the waves I slew
nicors by night, in need and peril
avenging the Weders, whose woe they sought,—
crushing the grim ones. Grendel now,
monster cruel, be mine to quell
in single battle! So, from thee,
thou sovran of the Shining-Danes,
Scyldings'-bulwark, a boon I seek,—
and, Friend-of-the-folk, refuse it not,
O Warriors'-shield, now I've wandered far,—
that I alone with my liegemen here,
this hardy band, may Heorot purge!
More I hear, that the monster dire,
in his wanton mood, of weapons recks not;

hence shall I scorn—so Hygelac stay,
king of my kindred, kind to me!—
brand or buckler to bear in the fight,
gold-colored targe: but with gripe alone
must I front the fiend and fight for life,
foe against foe. Then faith be his
in the doom of the Lord whom death shall take.
Fain, I ween, if the fight he win,
in this hall of gold my Geatish band
will he fearless eat,—as oft before,—
my noblest thanes. Nor need'st thou then
to hide my head; for his shall I be,
dyed in gore, if death must take me;
and my blood-covered body he'll bear as prey,
ruthless devour it, the roamer-lonely,
with my life-blood redden his lair in the fen:
no further for me need'st food prepare!
To Hygelac send, if Hild should take me,
best of war-weeds, warding my breast,
armor excellent, heirloom of Hrethel
and work of Wayland. Fares Wyrd as she must."

Chapter 6

HROTHGAR answered, "I remember him when he was young. His father was Ecgtheow, who was married to the daughter of Hrethel the Geat. And now their brave son comes to help his loyal friend. I once sent some sailors to the Geats to deliver some gifts, and they returned with wonderful tales about this man. They say he is as strong as thirty men. Merciful God has sent him to save us from Grendel's horrors. I will reward him for his bravery. Tell them to come forward and let them know that they are most welcome here." Wulfgar went to the door of the hall and said, "My master sends you this message. He knows your family well and welcomes you here. You may approach him in your armor, but leave your shields and weapons behind."

Beowulf gathered several of his warriors and followed Wulfgar, leaving some men behind to guard the weapons. Approaching Hrothgar in his shining armor, Beowulf spoke. "Hail, Hrothgar! I am Hygelac's loyal subject and kinsman, and I have earned respect in his lands. Even there I have heard of Grendel's evil deeds. Sailors talk about how your great hall stands empty at night. So my wise men suggested that I come to you, Hrothgar, in hopes that my strength and bravery may help you. They have seen me return from battle covered in the blood of my enemies. I have captured and killed monsters on land and in the sea and have avenged and defended my people against foes who got what they deserved. And now I come to destroy Grendel. I ask for your permission to rid your hall of this fiend using only my men. I have heard that Grendel does not use weapons, so I intend to kill him with my bare hands and earn more glory in Hygelac's name. The Lord will decide who will live and who will die. If Grendel wins, it will be an awful sight. He will gorge himself on my brave men. My body will not be here to be buried. He will take it back to his lair and eat it there. If this happens, send my armor back to Hygelac. Fate works as it must."

Chapter 7

HROTHGAR spake, the Scyldings'-helmet:—
"For fight defensive, Friend my Beowulf,
to succor and save, thou hast sought us here.
Thy father's combat a feud enkindled
when Heatholaf with hand he slew
among the Wylfings; his Weder kin
for horror of fighting feared to hold him.
Fleeing, he sought our South-Dane folk,
over surge of ocean the Honor-Scyldings,
when first I was ruling the folk of Danes,
wielded, youthful, this widespread realm,
this hoard-hold of heroes. Heorogar was dead,
my elder brother, had breathed his last,
Healfdene's bairn: he was better than I!
Straightway the feud with fee I settled,
to the Wylfings sent, o'er watery ridges,
treasures olden: oaths he swore me.
Sore is my soul to say to any
of the race of man what ruth for me
in Heorot Grendel with hate hath wrought,
what sudden harryings. Hall-folk fail me,
my warriors wane; for Wyrd hath swept them
into Grendel's grasp. But God is able
this deadly foe from his deeds to turn!
Boasted full oft, as my beer they drank,
earls o'er the ale-cup, armed men,
that they would bide in the beer-hall here,
Grendel's attack with terror of blades.
Then was this mead-house at morning tide
dyed with gore, when the daylight broke,
all the boards of the benches blood-besprinkled,
gory the hall: I had heroes the less,

doughty dear-ones that death had reft.
—But sit to the banquet, unbind thy words,
hardy hero, as heart shall prompt thee."

Gathered together, the Geatish men
in the banquet-hall on bench assigned,
sturdy-spirited, sat them down,
hardy-hearted. A henchman attended,
carried the carven cup in hand,
served the clear mead. Oft minstrels sang
blithe in Heorot. Heroes revelled,
no dearth of warriors, Weder and Dane.

Chapter 7

You have come here to defend us," Hrothgar replied. "Long ago your father started a feud when he killed Heatholaf of the Wylfings. Your father's people were afraid he would be killed in retaliation, so they sent him away. He sailed here. I had only recently become ruler of the Danes. My older brother Heorogar, a better man than I, had just died. I settled the feud by sending treasure to the Wylfings, and your father swore to be loyal to me. It is painful to me to trouble other people with the sufferings that Grendel has caused here in Heorot. But fate sweeps my men into Grendel's grasp, and only God can stop these evil deeds. Many times men have come here, sat at my banquet table, have drunk my ale, and claimed that they would stop Grendel, and every time my hall has wound up covered in their blood. Now it is your turn to sit at my table."

Beowulf and his strong-hearted men sat down in the banquet hall. A servant brought them beer. A minstrel sang and raised everyone's spirits.

Chapter 8

UNFERTH spake, the son of Ecglaf,
who sat at the feet of the Scyldings' lord,
unbound the battle-runes.—Beowulf's quest,
sturdy seafarer's, sorely galled him;
ever he envied that other men
should more achieve in middle-earth
of fame under heaven than he himself.—
"Art thou that Beowulf, Breca's rival,
who emulous swam on the open sea,
when for pride the pair of you proved the floods,
and wantonly dared in waters deep
to risk your lives? No living man,
or lief or loath, from your labor dire
could you dissuade, from swimming the main.
Ocean-tides with your arms ye covered,
with strenuous hands the sea-streets measured,
swam o'er the waters. Winter's storm
rolled the rough waves. In realm of sea
a sennight strove ye. In swimming he topped thee,
had more of main! Him at morning-tide
billows bore to the Battling Reamas,
whence he hied to his home so dear
beloved of his liegemen, to land of Brondings,
fastness fair, where his folk he ruled,
town and treasure. In triumph o'er thee
Beanstan's bairn his boast achieved.
So ween I for thee a worse adventure
—though in buffet of battle thou brave hast been,
in struggle grim,—if Grendel's approach
thou darst await through the watch of night!"

* * *

Beowulf spake, bairn of Ecgtheow:—
"What a deal hast uttered, dear my Unferth,
drunken with beer, of Breca now,
told of his triumph! Truth I claim it,
that I had more of might in the sea
than any man else, more ocean-endurance.
We twain had talked, in time of youth,
and made our boast,—we were merely boys,
striplings still,—to stake our lives
far at sea: and so we performed it.
Naked swords, as we swam along,
we held in hand, with hope to guard us
against the whales. Not a whit from me
could he float afar o'er the flood of waves,
haste o'er the billows; nor him I abandoned.
Together we twain on the tides abode
five nights full till the flood divided us,
churning waves and chillest weather,
darkling night, and the northern wind
ruthless rushed on us: rough was the surge.
Now the wrath of the sea-fish rose apace;
yet me 'gainst the monsters my mailed coat,
hard and hand-linked, help afforded,—
battle-sark braided my breast to ward,
garnished with gold. There grasped me firm
and haled me to bottom the hated foe,
with grimmest gripe. 'Twas granted me, though,
to pierce the monster with point of sword,
with blade of battle: huge beast of the sea
was whelmed by the hurly through hand of mine."

Chapter 8

SITTING near the king's feet was a man named Unferth. He was jealous of Beowulf and his bravery. He wanted to be the one who earned the fame and glory of victory. So he said, "Are you the same Beowulf whose vanity led him to battle Breca in the open sea just to show you could win? No one could stop you from swimming out after him. There was a terrible storm and you fought for seven nights, but in the end Breca came ashore the victor. He went back to his people confident in his superiority. You may be brave, but it won't matter now—no one has lasted even one night against Grendel."

Beowulf replied, "That's quite a tale you've told about Breca and me. I think the beer must be going to your head. If you want to know the truth, I was the stronger swimmer. Breca and I had talked about having a swimming contest like that since we were young children. We swam holding swords to protect ourselves from the sea beasts. Neither of us could gain the lead. We swam next to each other for five nights until a rough sea split us apart. The storm awakened the creatures of the deep. A sea monster pulled me down to the bottom, but my armor protected me. I was able to stab the beast with my sword and break free. The monsters kept attacking me. I drove them off again and again with my sword. I would not let them turn me into a feast at the bottom of the sea. I made sure that by morning they were washing up on the shore. I made that stretch of the ocean safe for sailors."

Chapter 9

ME thus often the evil monsters
thronging threatened. With thrust of my sword,
the darling, I dealt them due return!
Nowise had they bliss from their booty then
to devour their victim, vengeful creatures,
seated to banquet at bottom of sea;
but at break of day, by my brand sore hurt,
on the edge of ocean up they lay,
put to sleep by the sword. And since, by them
on the fathomless sea-ways sailor-folk
are never molested.—Light from east,
came bright God's beacon; the billows sank,
so that I saw the sea-cliffs high,
windy walls. For Wyrd oft saveth
earl undoomed if he doughty be!
And so it came that I killed with my sword
nine of the nicors. Of night-fought battles
ne'er heard I a harder 'neath heaven's dome,
nor adrift on the deep a more desolate man!
Yet I came unharmed from that hostile clutch,
though spent with swimming. The sea upbore me,
flood of the tide, on Finnish land,
the welling waters. No wise of thee
have I heard men tell such terror of falchions,
bitter battle. Breca ne'er yet,
not one of you pair, in the play of war
such daring deed has done at all
with bloody brand,—I boast not of it!—
though thou wast the bane of thy brethren dear,
thy closest kin, whence curse of hell
awaits thee, well as thy wit may serve!
For I say in sooth, thou son of Ecglaf,

never had Grendel these grim deeds wrought,
monster dire, on thy master dear,
in Heorot such havoc, if heart of thine
were as battle-bold as thy boast is loud!
But he has found no feud will happen;
from sword-clash dread of your Danish clan
he vaunts him safe, from the Victor-Scyldings.
He forces pledges, favors none
of the land of Danes, but lustily murders,
fights and feasts, nor feud he dreads
from Spear-Dane men. But speedily now
shall I prove him the prowess and pride of the Geats,
shall bid him battle. Blithe to mead
go he that listeth, when light of dawn
this morrow morning o'er men of earth,
ether-robed sun from the south shall beam!"

Joyous then was the Jewel-giver,
hoar-haired, war-brave; help awaited
the Bright-Danes' prince, from Beowulf hearing,
folk's good shepherd, such firm resolve.
Then was laughter of liegemen loud resounding
with winsome words. Came Wealtheow forth,
queen of Hrothgar, heedful of courtesy,
gold-decked, greeting the guests in hall;
and the high-born lady handed the cup
first to the East-Danes' heir and warden,
bade him be blithe at the beer-carouse,
the land's beloved one. Lustily took he
banquet and beaker, battle-famed king.

Through the hall then went the Helmings' Lady,
to younger and older everywhere
carried the cup, till come the moment

when the ring-graced queen, the royal-hearted,
to Beowulf bore the beaker of mead.
She greeted the Geats' lord, God she thanked,
in wisdom's words, that her will was granted,
that at last on a hero her hope could lean
for comfort in terrors. The cup he took,
hardy-in-war, from Wealtheow's hand,
and answer uttered the eager-for-combat.
Beowulf spake, bairn of Ecgtheow:—
"This was my thought, when my thanes and I
bent to the ocean and entered our boat,
that I would work the will of your people
fully, or fighting fall in death,
in fiend's gripe fast. I am firm to do
an earl's brave deed, or end the days
of this life of mine in the mead-hall here."
Well these words to the woman seemed,
Beowulf's battle-boast.—Bright with gold
the stately dame by her spouse sat down.
Again, as erst, began in hall
warriors' wassail and words of power,
the proud-band's revel, till presently
the son of Healfdene hastened to seek
rest for the night; he knew there waited
fight for the fiend in that festal hall,
when the sheen of the sun they saw no more,
and dusk of night sank darkling nigh,
and shadowy shapes came striding on,
wan under welkin. The warriors rose.
Man to man, he made harangue,
Hrothgar to Beowulf, bade him hail,
let him wield the wine hall: a word he added:—
"Never to any man erst I trusted,
since I could heave up hand and shield,

this noble Dane-Hall, till now to thee.
Have now and hold this house unpeered;
remember thy glory; thy might declare;
watch for the foe! No wish shall fail thee
if thou bidest the battle with bold-won life."

Chapter 9

SOON it was morning and God's light was shining from the east. I saw high cliffs nearby. Fate saves those who are brave. I had killed nine sea monsters. I've never heard of another man who fought such a battle. I was exhausted, but I was alive. I was swept ashore on a beach in Finland. I've never heard of you fighting such a battle, Unferth. It's not bragging on my part to say that neither you nor Breca can match up to me with a sword. You are responsible for the deaths of your family and will pay for it in hell. If you were really so brave and fierce, Unferth, Grendel wouldn't still be killing everyone in Heorot. He knows he has nothing to fear from your sword, that you aren't brave enough to fight him. He just goes on killing and feasting. The Danes are no match for him. But I will show him the power of the Geats. And then no one will be afraid to enter the mead hall in the morning."

Hrothgar was overjoyed at this speech. He knew help had truly arrived. Everyone grew happy afterward, and their talk and laughter filled the hall. Hrothgar's wife, Queen Wealtheow, came into the hall to greet the guests. She was dressed in gold. She handed her husband the ale cup and told him to drink first, since he was dear to his people. He gulped it down.

Then she took the cup from man to man so that each could drink. At last she arrived at Beowulf. She welcomed him and thanked God that her prayers were answered. Beowulf took the cup and spoke to everyone. "When my men and I set out for this place, I told myself that I would do my best for you and your people or die trying. I am determined to prove my bravery or end my life here in this hall." Beowulf's speech pleased Wealtheow, who went and sat down next to her husband. A festive mood returned to the hall. The joyful atmosphere lasted until Hrothgar got up and prepared to leave for the night. Grendel would be coming soon. The foul monster had waited all day to return for his nightly horror, but tonight he would have a fight waiting for him. The warriors stood up as Beowulf and Hrothgar said goodnight. "I have never entrusted my hall to anyone else before tonight," Hrothgar said, "but I believe in you. Protect this great hall, watch for your enemy, and remember that you fight for eternal glory. If you are victorious, you will have everything that you desire."

Chapter 10

THEN Hrothgar went with his hero-train,
defence-of-Scyldings, forth from hall;
fain would the war-lord Wealtheow seek,
couch of his queen. The King-of-Glory
against this Grendel a guard had set,
so heroes heard, a hall-defender,
who warded the monarch and watched for the monster.
In truth, the Geats' prince gladly trusted
his mettle, his might, the mercy of God!
Cast off then his corselet of iron,
helmet from head; to his henchman gave,—
choicest of weapons,—the well-chased sword,
bidding him guard the gear of battle.
Spake then his Vaunt the valiant man,
Beowulf Geat, ere the bed be sought:—
"Of force in fight no feebler I count me,
in grim war-deeds, than Grendel deems him.
Not with the sword, then, to sleep of death
his life will I give, though it lie in my power.
No skill is his to strike against me,
my shield to hew though he hardy be,
bold in battle; we both, this night,
shall spurn the sword, if he seek me here,
unweaponed, for war. Let wisest God,
sacred Lord, on which side soever
doom decree as he deemeth right."
Reclined then the chieftain, and cheek-pillows held
the head of the earl, while all about him
seamen hardy on hall-beds sank.
None of them thought that thence their steps
to the folk and fastness that fostered them,
to the land they loved, would lead them back!

Beowulf

Full well they wist that on warriors many
battle-death seized, in the banquet-hall,
of Danish clan. But comfort and help,
war-weal weaving, to Weder folk
the Master gave, that, by might of one,
over their enemy all prevailed,
by single strength. In sooth 'tis told
that highest God o'er human kind
hath wielded ever!—Thro' wan night striding,
came the walker-in-shadow. Warriors slept
whose hest was to guard the gabled hall,—
all save one. 'Twas widely known
that against God's will the ghostly ravager
him could not hurl to haunts of darkness;
wakeful, ready, with warrior's wrath,
bold he bided the battle's issue.

Chapter 10

HROTHGAR left with his royal guard. He knew his hall was safe because God, the King of Glory, had put Beowulf there to protect it from Grendel. And Beowulf put his faith in God and his own strength. So he removed his helmet and armor and handed his best sword to his servant with orders to take care of it. Before he went to sleep, Beowulf spoke to his men. "I consider myself as fierce a fighter as Grendel. So I will fight him by hand, not with a sword, and I will still win. Grendel does not use a sword or shield. He relies only on his strength. And so will I. If he comes for me, we will battle, and God will decide the victor." They all went to bed. There wasn't a man among them who was sure that he would see his home again. They knew how many Danish warriors had already died in this hall. But God was preparing a victory for the Geats. They would win because all of their strength would be found in one man. God's will always rules over men.

Chapter 11

THEN from the moorland, by misty crags,
with God's wrath laden, Grendel came.
The monster was minded of mankind now
sundry to seize in the stately house.
Under welkin he walked, till the wine-palace there,
gold-hall of men, he gladly discerned,
flashing with fretwork. Not first time, this,
that he the home of Hrothgar sought,—
yet ne'er in his life-day, late or early,
such hardy heroes, such hall-thanes, found!
To the house the warrior walked apace,
parted from peace; the portal opended,
though with forged bolts fast, when his fists had struck it,
and baleful he burst in his blatant rage,
the house's mouth. All hastily, then,
o'er fair-paved floor the fiend trod on,
ireful he strode; there streamed from his eyes
fearful flashes, like flame to see.

He spied in hall the hero-band,
kin and clansmen clustered asleep,
hardy liegemen. Then laughed his heart;
for the monster was minded, ere morn should dawn,
savage, to sever the soul of each,
life from body, since lusty banquet
waited his will! But Wyrd forbade him
to seize any more of men on earth
after that evening. Eagerly watched
Hygelac's kinsman his cursed foe,
how he would fare in fell attack.
Not that the monster was minded to pause!
Straightway he seized a sleeping warrior

for the first, and tore him fiercely asunder,
the bone-frame bit, drank blood in streams,
swallowed him piecemeal: swiftly thus
the lifeless corse was clear devoured,
e'en feet and hands. Then farther he hied;
for the hardy hero with hand he grasped,
felt for the foe with fiendish claw,
for the hero reclining,—who clutched it boldly,
prompt to answer, propped on his arm.
Soon then saw that shepherd-of-evils
that never he met in this middle-world,
in the ways of earth, another wight
with heavier hand-gripe; at heart he feared,
sorrowed in soul,—none the sooner escaped!
Fain would he flee, his fastness seek,
the den of devils: no doings now
such as oft he had done in days of old!

Then bethought him the hardy Hygelac-thane
of his boast at evening: up he bounded,
grasped firm his foe, whose fingers cracked.
The fiend made off, but the earl close followed.
The monster meant—if he might at all—
to fling himself free, and far away
fly to the fens,—knew his fingers' power
in the gripe of the grim one. Gruesome march
to Heorot this monster of harm had made!
Din filled the room; the Danes were bereft,
castle-dwellers and clansmen all,
earls, of their ale. Angry were both
those savage hall-guards: the house resounded.
Wonder it was the wine-hall firm
in the strain of their struggle stood, to earth
the fair house fell not; too fast it was

within and without by its iron bands
craftily clamped; though there crashed from sill
many a mead-bench—men have told me—
gay with gold, where the grim foes wrestled.
So well had weened the wisest Scyldings
that not ever at all might any man
that bone-decked, brave house break asunder,
crush by craft,—unless clasp of fire
in smoke engulfed it.—Again uprose
din redoubled. Danes of the North
with fear and frenzy were filled, each one,
who from the wall that wailing heard,
God's foe sounding his grisly song,
cry of the conquered, clamorous pain
from captive of hell. Too closely held him
he who of men in might was strongest
in that same day of this our life.

Chapter 11

NIGHT fell. The one who walks in shadows was coming to them. All of the hall guards were asleep except for one. The one who was awake was ready for the fiend. Grendel stalked through the misty swamps, making his way to the great hall. He walked in the shadows until at last he arrived. He had come here many times, but never had he faced such powerful enemies. He tore open the door and strode in, his eyes aflame with rage.

He saw the Geats asleep on the floor and he laughed to himself. Before morning he planned to kill and eat them all. Fate, however, had other plans for Grendel. Beowulf was carefully watching the monster, waiting for him to attack. He didn't have to wait long. Grendel grabbed a sleeping man and broke him open. He crushed the man's bones and drank his blood. When he was finished, he turned toward Beowulf and raised his terrible claw to strike. But Beowulf struck first, grabbing the monster's claw in his powerful hand. Grendel had never felt such strength in a man before. For the first time, he was afraid. He wanted to return to his foul den and hide there.

Beowulf remembered the promise he had made, so he leapt up and grabbed Grendel tighter, breaking the beast's fingers. Grendel pulled free and tried to run, but Beowulf followed. Everyone was awake now and the hall was in chaos. Grendel and Beowulf crashed around the room, turning over benches and smashing into the walls. The hall shook, but it stood. The Danes could hardly believe their eyes—they thought only fire could cause this much damage to their hall. A terrifying wail echoed through the hall. The Danes could feel the scream in their bones. It was Grendel's cry. He was wounded and Beowulf had him firmly in his grip.

Chapter 12

NOT in any wise would the earls'-defence
suffer that slaughterous stranger to live,
useless deeming his days and years
to men on earth. Now many an earl
of Beowulf brandished blade ancestral,
fain the life of their lord to shield,
their praised prince, if power were theirs;
never they knew,—as they neared the foe,
hardy-hearted heroes of war,
aiming their swords on every side
the accursed to kill,—no keenest blade,
no farest of falchions fashioned on earth,
could harm or hurt that hideous fiend!
He was safe, by his spells, from sword of battle,
from edge of iron. Yet his end and parting
on that same day of this our life
woful should be, and his wandering soul
far off flit to the fiends' domain.
Soon he found, who in former days,
harmful in heart and hated of God,
on many a man such murder wrought,
that the frame of his body failed him now.
For him the keen-souled kinsman of Hygelac
held in hand; hateful alive
was each to other. The outlaw dire
took mortal hurt; a mighty wound
showed on his shoulder, and sinews cracked,
and the bone-frame burst. To Beowulf now
the glory was given, and Grendel thence
death-sick his den in the dark moor sought,
noisome abode: he knew too well
that here was the last of life, an end

of his days on earth.—To all the Danes
by that bloody battle the boon had come.
From ravage had rescued the roving stranger
Hrothgar's hall; the hardy and wise one
had purged it anew. His night-work pleased him,
his deed and its honor. To Eastern Danes
had the valiant Geat his vaunt made good,
all their sorrow and ills assuaged,
their bale of battle borne so long,
and all the dole they erst endured
pain a-plenty.—'Twas proof of this,
when the hardy-in-fight a hand laid down,
arm and shoulder,—all, indeed,
of Grendel's gripe,—'neath the gabled roof.

Chapter 12

BEOWULF was determined not to let Grendel live. His men kept trying to help him, striking out at the foul fiend with their swords. They did not know that even the sharpest blade could not pierce Grendel's skin. The monster was protected by demonic spells that repelled any weapon. Yet he was nearing the end of his life. Grendel's strength was failing him. Beowulf wouldn't release his powerful grasp. They were locked in the grip of hatred. Grendel's whole body shook with pain as his shoulder began to come apart. His bones and muscles broke and tore, and Beowulf wrenched off his arm. It was a fatal wound, and Beowulf drove the monster out of the hall and back into the swamps. Grendel went to his foul den to die. The wishes of the Danes had come true. Beowulf had cleansed their hall of evil and saved them from death. He had made good on his promise and earned glory for his bravery. As a display of Beowulf's victory, Grendel's arm was mounted on the wall of the great hall.

Chapter 13

MANY at morning, as men have told me,
warriors gathered the gift-hall round,
folk-leaders faring from far and near,
o'er wide-stretched ways, the wonder to view,
trace of the traitor. Not troublous seemed
the enemy's end to any man
who saw by the gait of the graceless foe
how the weary-hearted, away from thence,
baffled in battle and banned, his steps
death-marked dragged to the devils' mere.
Bloody the billows were boiling there,
turbid the tide of tumbling waves
horribly seething, with sword-blood hot,
by that doomed one dyed, who in den of the moor
laid forlorn his life adown,
his heathen soul, and hell received it.

Home then rode the hoary clansmen
from that merry journey, and many a youth,
on horses white, the hardy warriors,
back from the mere. Then Beowulf's glory
eager they echoed, and all averred
that from sea to sea, or south or north,
there was no other in earth's domain,
under vault of heaven, more valiant found,
of warriors none more worthy to rule!
(On their lord beloved they laid no slight,
gracious Hrothgar: a good king he!)

From time to time, the tried-in-battle
their gray steeds set to gallop amain,
and ran a race when the road seemed fair.

Beowulf

From time to time, a thane of the king,
who had made many vaunts, and was mindful of verses,
stored with sagas and songs of old,
bound word to word in well-knit rime,
welded his lay; this warrior soon
of Beowulf's quest right cleverly sang,
and artfully added an excellent tale,
in well-ranged words, of the warlike deeds
he had heard in saga of Sigemund.
Strange the story: he said it all,—
the Waelsing's wanderings wide, his struggles,
which never were told to tribes of men,
the feuds and the frauds, save to Fitela only,
when of these doings he deigned to speak,
uncle to nephew; as ever the twain
stood side by side in stress of war,
and multitude of the monster kind
they had felled with their swords. Of Sigemund grew,
when he passed from life, no little praise;
for the doughty-in-combat a dragon killed
that herded the hoard: under hoary rock
the atheling dared the deed alone
fearful quest, nor was Fitela there.
Yet so it befell, his falchion pierced
that wondrous worm,—on the wall it struck,
best blade; the dragon died in its blood.
Thus had the dread-one by daring achieved
over the ring-hoard to rule at will,
himself to pleasure; a sea-boat he loaded,
and bore on its bosom the beaming gold,
son of Waels; the worm was consumed.
He had of all heroes the highest renown
among races of men, this refuge-of-warriors,
for deeds of daring that decked his name

Beowulf

since the hand and heart of Heremod
grew slack in battle. He, swiftly banished
to mingle with monsters at mercy of foes,
to death was betrayed; for torrents of sorrow
had lamed him too long; a load of care
to earls and athelings all he proved.
Oft indeed, in earlier days,
for the warrior's wayfaring wise men mourned,
who had hoped of him help from harm and bale,
and had thought their sovran's son would thrive,
follow his father, his folk protect,
the hoard and the stronghold, heroes' land,
home of Scyldings.—But here, thanes said,
the kinsman of Hygelac kinder seemed
to all: the other was urged to crime!

And afresh to the race, the fallow roads
by swift steeds measured! The morning sun
was climbing higher. Clansmen hastened
to the high-built hall, those hardy-minded,
the wonder to witness. Warden of treasure,
crowned with glory, the king himself,
with stately band from the bride-bower strode;
and with him the queen and her crowd of maidens
measured the path to the mead-house fair.

Chapter 13

As daylight broke, men from all over the country came to the hall. They were happy to see the tracks Grendel left behind as he fled to his den. The swamp was filled with his blood. As he neared death, he dove into the water and drowned himself, sending his soul to hell.

Throughout the land, people repeated the story of Beowulf's strength and bravery. Although people stayed loyal to their good king Hrothgar, it was said that no man deserved to rule more than the glorious Beowulf.

Hrothgar's minstrel came up with a new song, one praising Beowulf's triumph. He combined the story of Beowulf's deeds with those of the mythic hero Sigmund and his offspring, Fitela. Those two heroes of long ago killed many giants and other monsters. The minstrel told of how Sigmund killed a dragon all by himself and took the dragon's treasure. Like Beowulf, Sigmund was considered a great hero and his name was known throughout the land. Sigmund's fortunes grew after his king, Heremod, was overthrown and killed. Heremod did not protect his people like Beowulf had.

So all of the noble clansmen, including the great king himself and his queen, rode to the great hall to witness Beowulf's great deed.

Chapter 14

HROTHGAR spake,—to the hall he went,
stood by the steps, the steep roof saw,
garnished with gold, and Grendel's hand:—
"For the sight I see to the Sovran Ruler
be speedy thanks! A throng of sorrows
I have borne from Grendel; but God still works
wonder on wonder, the Warden-of-Glory.
It was but now that I never more
for woes that weighed on me waited help
long as I lived, when, laved in blood,
stood sword-gore-stained this stateliest house,—
widespread woe for wise men all,
who had no hope to hinder ever
foes infernal and fiendish sprites
from havoc in hall. This hero now,
by the Wielder's might, a work has done
that not all of us erst could ever do
by wile and wisdom. Lo, well can she say
whoso of women this warrior bore
among sons of men, if still she liveth,
that the God of the ages was good to her
in the birth of her bairn. Now, Beowulf, thee,
of heroes best, I shall heartily love
as mine own, my son; preserve thou ever
this kinship new: thou shalt never lack
wealth of the world that I wield as mine!
Full oft for less have I largess showered,
my precious hoard, on a punier man,
less stout in struggle. Thyself hast now
fulfilled such deeds, that thy fame shall endure
through all the ages. As ever he did,
well may the Wielder reward thee still!"
Beowulf spake, bairn of Ecgtheow:—

Beowulf

"This work of war most willingly
we have fought, this fight, and fearlessly dared
force of the foe. Fain, too, were I
hadst thou but seen himself, what time
the fiend in his trappings tottered to fall!
Swiftly, I thought, in strongest gripe
on his bed of death to bind him down,
that he in the hent of this hand of mine
should breathe his last: but he broke away.
Him I might not—the Maker willed not—
hinder from flight, and firm enough hold
the life-destroyer: too sturdy was he,
the ruthless, in running! For rescue, however,
he left behind him his hand in pledge,
arm and shoulder; nor aught of help
could the cursed one thus procure at all.
None the longer liveth he, loathsome fiend,
sunk in his sins, but sorrow holds him
tightly grasped in gripe of anguish,
in baleful bonds, where bide he must,
evil outlaw, such awful doom
as the Mighty Maker shall mete him out."

More silent seemed the son of Ecglaf
in boastful speech of his battle-deeds,
since athelings all, through the earl's great prowess,
beheld that hand, on the high roof gazing,
foeman's fingers,—the forepart of each
of the sturdy nails to steel was likest,—
heathen's "hand-spear," hostile warrior's
claw uncanny. 'Twas clear, they said,
that him no blade of the brave could touch,
how keen soever, or cut away
that battle-hand bloody from baneful foe.

Chapter 14

MORE and more men rode their horses to the great hall to see what Beowulf had done. The king and his queen left their private quarters and came into the hall. There, Hrothgar looked up at Grendel's arm, mounted on the wall, and gave a speech. "First, let us thank Almighty God for this sight. I have long suffered at the hands of Grendel, but God has delivered us from that monster's grasp. I thought I would never be rid of that foul beast and the sorrows he caused. This glorious hall was filled with blood night after night. But now one man, with God's help, has done what all of us together could not do. If his mother is still alive, she can thank God for the great gift He gave her. Now, Beowulf, I will love you as my own son. Take this bond seriously. You will have everything that wealth can provide. In the past I have given honor and riches to men who have achieved much less than you have. But your honor will live forever. May God protect and bless you." Beowulf replied, "We fought this battle willingly and were blessed with victory. I wish that his whole body was still here so you could see the fiend where he fell. That was my plan, but he broke free and died in his den. God willed it this way. But the beast left behind his arm and cannot live long. He must suffer the punishment God has planned for him."

Unferth, who had been so boastful the day before, now sat silently. Everyone could see the proof of Beowulf's power hanging on the wall. Grendel's claw was as hard as steel, and it was obvious that no sword could have severed his arm from his body.

Chapter 15

THERE was hurry and hest in Heorot now
 for hands to bedeck it, and dense was the throng
of men and women the wine-hall to cleanse,
the guest-room to garnish. Gold-gay shone the hangings
that were wove on the wall, and wonders many
to delight each mortal that looks upon them.
Though braced within by iron bands,
that building bright was broken sorely;
rent were its hinges; the roof alone
held safe and sound, when, seared with crime,
the fiendish foe his flight essayed,
of life despairing.—No light thing that,
the flight for safety,—essay it who will!
Forced of fate, he shall find his way
to the refuge ready for race of man,
for soul-possessors, and sons of earth;
and there his body on bed of death
shall rest after revel.
Arrived was the hour
when to hall proceeded Healfdene's son:
the king himself would sit to banquet.
Ne'er heard I of host in haughtier throng
more graciously gathered round giver-of-rings!
Bowed then to bench those bearers-of-glory,
fain of the feasting. Featly received
many a mead-cup the mighty-in-spirit,
kinsmen who sat in the sumptuous hall,
Hrothgar and Hrothulf. Heorot now
was filled with friends; the folk of Scyldings
ne'er yet had tried the traitor's deed.

Beowulf

***

To Beowulf gave the bairn of Healfdene
a gold-wove banner, guerdon of triumph,
broidered battle-flag, breastplate and helmet;
and a splendid sword was seen of many
borne to the brave one. Beowulf took
cup in hall: for such costly gifts
he suffered no shame in that soldier throng.
For I heard of few heroes, in heartier mood,
with four such gifts, so fashioned with gold,
on the ale-bench honoring others thus!
O'er the roof of the helmet high, a ridge,
wound with wires, kept ward o'er the head,
lest the relict-of-files should fierce invade,
sharp in the strife, when that shielded hero
should go to grapple against his foes.
Then the earls'-defence on the floor bade lead
coursers eight, with carven head-gear,
adown the hall: one horse was decked
with a saddle all shining and set in jewels;
'twas the battle-seat of the best of kings,
when to play of swords the son of Healfdene
was fain to fare. Ne'er failed his valor
in the crush of combat when corpses fell.
To Beowulf over them both then gave
the refuge-of-Ingwines right and power,
o'er war-steeds and weapons: wished him joy of them.
Manfully thus the mighty prince,
hoard-guard for heroes, that hard fight repaid
with steeds and treasures contemned by none
who is willing to say the sooth aright.

Chapter 15

E VERYONE began to pitch in to help repair the damage done to Heorot and to prepare it for a feast. Wonderful new decorations were to be hung from the walls. Though the building still stood, it was badly damaged by the battle. The roof was the only part that wasn't scarred by Grendel's attack and his attempt to escape. No one, however, can escape death—it awaits us all. It was time for Hrothgar to arrive at the banquet. Never before did such a large and noble group gather around their king. Famous men from across the land sat at the tables, drinking endless rounds of mead. Everyone in Heorot was filled with the spirit of friendship. The people had not yet learned to betray one another.

Hrothgar gave Beowulf a splendid new sword and set of armor, along with a golden battle flag and a helmet with a ridge to protect its wearer. Beowulf drank to his host. He was not ashamed to receive such expensive gifts in front of his men, for he had earned them. It is rare that treasures like those would be handed over in so friendly a way. Then Hrothgar had eight horses brought into the hall. One was wearing a saddle covered in gold and jewels. It was the saddle Hrothgar used when he rode bravely into battle. He gave this all to Beowulf. The king behaved very nobly.

Chapter 16

A ND the lord of earls, to each that came
with Beowulf over the briny ways,
an heirloom there at the ale-bench gave,
precious gift; and the price bade pay
in gold for him whom Grendel erst
murdered,—and fain of them more had killed,
had not wisest God their Wyrd averted,
and the man's brave mood. The Maker then
ruled human kind, as here and now.
Therefore is insight always best,
and forethought of mind. How much awaits him
of lief and of loath, who long time here,
through days of warfare this world endures!

Then song and music mingled sounds
in the presence of Healfdene's head-of-armies
and harping was heard with the hero-lay
as Hrothgar's singer the hall-joy woke
along the mead-seats, making his song
of that sudden raid on the sons of Finn.

Healfdene's hero, Hnaef the Scylding,
was fated to fall in the Frisian slaughter.
Hildeburh needed not hold in value
her enemies' honor! Innocent both
were the loved ones she lost at the linden-play,
bairn and brother, they bowed to fate,
stricken by spears; 'twas a sorrowful woman!
None doubted why the daughter of Hoc
bewailed her doom when dawning came,
and under the sky she saw them lying,
kinsmen murdered, where most she had kenned

Beowulf

of the sweets of the world! By war were swept, too,
Finn's own liegemen, and few were left;
in the parleying-place he could ply no longer
weapon, nor war could he wage on Hengest,
and rescue his remnant by right of arms
from the prince's thane. A pact he offered:
another dwelling the Danes should have,
hall and high-seat, and half the power
should fall to them in Frisian land;
and at the fee-gifts, Folcwald's son
day by day the Danes should honor,
the folk of Hengest favor with rings,
even as truly, with treasure and jewels,
with fretted gold, as his Frisian kin
he meant to honor in ale-hall there.
Pact of peace they plighted further
on both sides firmly. Finn to Hengest
with oath, upon honor, openly promised
that woful remnant, with wise-men's aid,
nobly to govern, so none of the guests
by word or work should warp the treaty,
or with malice of mind bemoan themselves
as forced to follow their fee-giver's slayer,
lordless men, as their lot ordained.
Should Frisian, moreover, with foeman's taunt,
that murderous hatred to mind recall,
then edge of the sword must seal his doom.
Oaths were given, and ancient gold
heaped from hoard.—The hardy Scylding,
battle-thane best, on his balefire lay.
All on the pyre were plain to see
the gory sark, the gilded swine-crest,
boar of hard iron, and athelings many
slain by the sword: at the slaughter they fell.

Beowulf

It was Hildeburh's hest, at Hnaef's own pyre
the bairn of her body on brands to lay,
his bones to burn, on the balefire placed,
at his uncle's side. In sorrowful dirges
bewept them the woman: great wailing ascended.
Then wound up to welkin the wildest of death-fires,
roared o'er the hillock: heads all were melted,
gashes burst, and blood gushed out
from bites of the body. Balefire devoured,
greediest spirit, those spared not by war
out of either folk: their flower was gone.

Chapter 16

HROTHGAR also gave treasures to all of the men who had sailed with Beowulf and compensated them for the loss of the man Grendel killed. The monster would have killed more if it had not been for Beowulf's bravery and God's will. Because God's will always triumphs, the best thing anyone can do is seek to understand. There is so much that a person who lives a long life must endure.

There was much singing and harp-playing in the hall. The king's minstrel sang a song about the legendary ruler Finn and his sons. Finn, who ruled the Frisians, was married to Hildeburh, the sister of Hnaef, ruler of the Scyldings of Denmark.

Hnaef was killed during a battle with the Frisians, as was Hildeburh's son. Hengest, Hnaef's second-in-command, agreed to a truce with the Frisians. The terms of the truce meant that Finn had to give Hengest and the other Scyldings the same treasures he gave his own people, and he had to house them for a time, as they could not return to Denmark in the winter. Hildeburh insisted that the body of Hnaef and her son be burned on the same pyre, and she wept over them as the fire consumed their bodies.

Chapter 17

THEN hastened those heroes their home to see,
friendless, to find the Frisian land,
houses and high burg. Hengest still
through the death-dyed winter dwelt with Finn,
holding pact, yet of home he minded,
though powerless his ring-decked prow to drive
over the waters, now waves rolled fierce
lashed by the winds, or winter locked them
in icy fetters. Then fared another
year to men's dwellings, as yet they do,
the sunbright skies, that their season ever
duly await. Far off winter was driven;
fair lay earth's breast; and fain was the rover,
the guest, to depart, though more gladly he pondered
on wreaking his vengeance than roaming the deep,
and how to hasten the hot encounter
where sons of the Frisians were sure to be.
So he escaped not the common doom,
when Hun with "Lafing," the light-of-battle,
best of blades, his bosom pierced:
its edge was famed with the Frisian earls.
On fierce-heart Finn there fell likewise,
on himself at home, the horrid sword-death;
for Guthlaf and Oslaf of grim attack
had sorrowing told, from sea-ways landed,
mourning their woes. Finn's wavering spirit
bode not in breast. The burg was reddened
with blood of foemen, and Finn was slain,
king amid clansmen; the queen was taken.
To their ship the Scylding warriors bore
all the chattels the chieftain owned,
whatever they found in Finn's domain
of gems and jewels. The gentle wife

o'er paths of the deep to the Danes they bore,
led to her land.
The lay was finished,
the gleeman's song. Then glad rose the revel;
bench-joy brightened. Bearers draw
from their "wonder-vats" wine. Comes Wealtheow forth,
under gold-crown goes where the good pair sit,
uncle and nephew, true each to the other one,
kindred in amity. Unferth the spokesman
at the Scylding lord's feet sat: men had faith in his spirit,
his keenness of courage, though kinsmen had found him
unsure at the sword-play. The Scylding queen spoke:
"Quaff of this cup, my king and lord,
breaker of rings, and blithe be thou,
gold-friend of men; to the Geats here speak
such words of mildness as man should use.
Be glad with thy Geats; of those gifts be mindful,
or near or far, which now thou hast.
Men say to me, as son thou wishest
yon hero to hold. Thy Heorot purged,
jewel-hall brightest, enjoy while thou canst,
with many a largess; and leave to thy kin
folk and realm when forth thou goest
to greet thy doom. For gracious I deem
my Hrothulf, willing to hold and rule
nobly our youths, if thou yield up first,
prince of Scyldings, thy part in the world.
I ween with good he will well requite
offspring of ours, when all he minds
that for him we did in his helpless days
of gift and grace to gain him honor!"
Then she turned to the seat where her sons were placed,
Hrethric and Hrothmund, with heroes' bairns,
young men together: the Geat, too, sat there,
Beowulf brave, the brothers between.

Chapter 17

AND so the Danish heroes went to live among the Frisians. Hengest kept the pact with Finn through the fierce winter, since he was unable to sail back home. Spring approached and Hengest prepared his men for their departure, but he still harbored vengeful thoughts. The Danes grew restless and eventually they killed Finn and took Hildeburh back to Denmark. The minstrel finished his song. The sounds of talking and laughter returned to the hall. Queen Wealtheow came out and sat near her husband and Hrothulf, his nephew and advisor. Unferth was also nearby. Though he had a stain on his reputation, many people still respected Unferth for his mind and his courage. Wealtheow said to Hrothgar, "Drink up, my lord, and be happy. Treat the Geats well and enjoy your time with them. Be grateful for the gifts you have. Heorot has been saved and cleansed of evil. I have heard that you want to adopt Beowulf as your son. You are free to do so. You should give your kingdom to your family when you die. I have faith in your nephew Hrothulf. He will take care of our sons. If you die before he does, he will be good to them. He will remember everything that you have done for him." She looked over at her sons, Hrethric and Hrothmund, and saw Beowulf sitting between them.

Chapter 18

A cup she gave him, with kindly greeting
and winsome words. Of wounden gold,
she offered, to honor him, arm-jewels twain,
corselet and rings, and of collars the noblest
that ever I knew the earth around.
Ne'er heard I so mighty, 'neath heaven's dome,
a hoard-gem of heroes, since Hama bore
to his bright-built burg the Brisings' necklace,
jewel and gem casket.—Jealousy fled he,
Eormenric's hate: chose help eternal.
Hygelac Geat, grandson of Swerting,
on the last of his raids this ring bore with him,
under his banner the booty defending,
the war-spoil warding; but Wyrd o'erwhelmed him
what time, in his daring, dangers he sought,
feud with Frisians. Fairest of gems
he bore with him over the beaker-of-waves,
sovran strong: under shield he died.
Fell the corpse of the king into keeping of Franks,
gear of the breast, and that gorgeous ring;
weaker warriors won the spoil,
after gripe of battle, from Geatland's lord,
and held the death-field.
Din rose in hall.

Wealtheow spake amid warriors, and said:—
"This jewel enjoy in thy jocund youth,
Beowulf lov'd, these battle-weeds wear,
a royal treasure, and richly thrive!
Preserve thy strength, and these striplings here
counsel in kindness: requital be mine.

Beowulf

Hast done such deeds, that for days to come
thou art famed among folk both far and near,
so wide as washeth the wave of Ocean
his windy walls. Through the ways of life
prosper, O prince! I pray for thee
rich possessions. To son of mine
be helpful in deed and uphold his joys!
Here every earl to the other is true,
mild of mood, to the master loyal!
Thanes are friendly, the throng obedient,
liegemen are revelling: list and obey!"

Went then to her place.—That was proudest of feasts;
flowed wine for the warriors. Wyrd they knew not,
destiny dire, and the doom to be seen
by many an earl when eve should come,
and Hrothgar homeward hasten away,
royal, to rest. The room was guarded
by an army of earls, as erst was done.
They bared the bench-boards; abroad they spread
beds and bolsters.—One beer-carouser
in danger of doom lay down in the hall.—

At their heads they set their shields of war,
bucklers bright; on the bench were there
over each atheling, easy to see,
the high battle-helmet, the haughty spear,
the corselet of rings. 'Twas their custom so
ever to be for battle prepared,
at home, or harrying, which it were,
even as oft as evil threatened
their sovran king.—They were clansmen good.

Chapter 18

WEALTHEOW sent a cup of mead to Beowulf. She also gave him a gift of gold jewelry and a suit of chain mail. In later years, Beowulf gave the necklace to his uncle Hygelac, who was wearing it when he died in battle against the Frisians. There was much applause at Wealtheow's gift.

Wealtheow then spoke to Beowulf. "Enjoy these gifts, our beloved Beowulf, and may they keep you safe. Be strong and be a good guide to my sons. Your deeds have ensured that you will be remembered forever. I pray for your continued success, dear prince. Treat my sons well. We are all good to each other here and loyal to our king. They are friendly and they know their duty."

The queen went back to her seat. The feast was a grand one. The men gathered there did not know that fate was preparing another grim threat for them. Evening fell and Hrothgar headed home to sleep. The room was guarded as usual. The benches were pushed back and men made their beds on the floor. One reveler slept, not knowing that danger waited for him.

They slept with their shields and weapons nearby, so that they could be ready for battle whenever it came.

Chapter 19

THEN sank they to sleep. With sorrow one bought
his rest of the evening,—as ofttime had happened
when Grendel guarded that golden hall,
evil wrought, till his end drew nigh,
slaughter for sins. 'Twas seen and told
how an avenger survived the fiend,
as was learned afar. The livelong time
after that grim fight, Grendel's mother,
monster of women, mourned her woe.
She was doomed to dwell in the dreary waters,
cold sea-courses, since Cain cut down
with edge of the sword his only brother,
his father's offspring: outlawed he fled,
marked with murder, from men's delights
warded the wilds.—There woke from him
such fate-sent ghosts as Grendel, who,
war-wolf horrid, at Heorot found
a warrior watching and waiting the fray,
with whom the grisly one grappled amain.
But the man remembered his mighty power,
the glorious gift that God had sent him,
in his Maker's mercy put his trust
for comfort and help: so he conquered the foe,
felled the fiend, who fled abject,
reft of joy, to the realms of death,
mankind's foe. And his mother now,
gloomy and grim, would go that quest
of sorrow, the death of her son to avenge.
To Heorot came she, where helmeted Danes
slept in the hall. Too soon came back
old ills of the earls, when in she burst,
the mother of Grendel. Less grim, though, that terror,

Beowulf

e'en as terror of woman in war is less,
might of maid, than of men in arms
when, hammer-forged, the falchion hard,
sword gore-stained, through swine of the helm,
crested, with keen blade carves amain.
Then was in hall the hard-edge drawn,
the swords on the settles, and shields a-many
firm held in hand: nor helmet minded
nor harness of mail, whom that horror seized.

Haste was hers; she would hie afar
and save her life when the liegemen saw her.
Yet a single atheling up she seized
fast and firm, as she fled to the moor.
He was for Hrothgar of heroes the dearest,
of trusty vassals betwixt the seas,
whom she killed on his couch, a clansman famous,
in battle brave.—Nor was Beowulf there;
another house had been held apart,
after giving of gold, for the Geat renowned.—
Uproar filled Heorot; the hand all had viewed,
blood-flecked, she bore with her; bale was returned,
dole in the dwellings: 'twas dire exchange
where Dane and Geat were doomed to give
the lives of loved ones. Long-tried king,
the hoary hero, at heart was sad
when he knew his noble no more lived,
and dead indeed was his dearest thane.
To his bower was Beowulf brought in haste,
dauntless victor. As daylight broke,
along with his earls the atheling lord,
with his clansmen, came where the king abode
waiting to see if the Wielder-of-All
would turn this tale of trouble and woe.

Strode o'er floor the famed-in-strife,
with his hand-companions,—the hall resounded,—
wishing to greet the wise old king,
Ingwines' lord; he asked if the night
had passed in peace to the prince's mind.

Chapter 19

THEY went to sleep, though one of them would not wake. Someone was seeking revenge for Grendel's death. Deep within the swamp, Grendel's mother had been mourning her son and waiting for vengeance. She had been doomed to live in the swamp ever since Cain killed Abel and was banished by God. Cain was the father of many evil beasts, including Grendel, whom brave Beowulf had killed with the help of God. And now Grendel's mother, driven by sorrow and rage, was coming for them. She came to Heorot, where the Danes were sleeping. She burst in with a woman's terrifying strength, only slightly less than Grendel's. Men leapt to their feet and grabbed their shields and swords.

As soon as she realized she had been discovered, she tried to escape. She grabbed one of the men, one of Hrothgar's closest friends, and rushed back to the swamp. Beowulf wasn't in the hall. He had been given a bed elsewhere. Heorot was in chaos. Grendel's mother had taken back her son's severed arm, in addition to the man she had grabbed. Hrothgar was devastated by the news. Beowulf was summoned to the king's side. Hrothgar had been wondering aloud whether God would ever stop this string of misfortunes. Beowulf strode in with his men and, not knowing what had happened, asked if Hrothgar had slept well.

Chapter 20

HROTHGAR spake, helmet-of-Scyldings:—
"Ask not of pleasure! Pain is renewed
to Danish folk. Dead is Aeschere,
of Yrmenlaf the elder brother,
my sage adviser and stay in council,
shoulder-comrade in stress of fight
when warriors clashed and we warded our heads,
hewed the helm-boars; hero famed
should be every earl as Aeschere was!
But here in Heorot a hand hath slain him
of wandering death-sprite. I wot not whither,
proud of the prey, her path she took,
fain of her fill. The feud she avenged
that yesternight, unyieldingly,
Grendel in grimmest grasp thou killedst,—
seeing how long these liegemen mine
he ruined and ravaged. Reft of life,
in arms he fell. Now another comes,
keen and cruel, her kin to avenge,
faring far in feud of blood:
so that many a thane shall think, who e'er
sorrows in soul for that sharer of rings,
this is hardest of heart-bales. The hand lies low
that once was willing each wish to please.
Land-dwellers here and liegemen mine,
who house by those parts, I have heard relate
that such a pair they have sometimes seen,
march-stalkers mighty the moorland haunting,
wandering spirits: one of them seemed,
so far as my folk could fairly judge,
of womankind; and one, accursed,
in man's guise trod the misery-track

of exile, though huger than human bulk.
Grendel in days long gone they named him,
folk of the land; his father they knew not,
nor any brood that was born to him
of treacherous spirits. Untrod is their home;
by wolf-cliffs haunt they and windy headlands,
fenways fearful, where flows the stream
from mountains gliding to gloom of the rocks,
underground flood. Not far is it hence
in measure of miles that the mere expands,
and o'er it the frost-bound forest hanging,
sturdily rooted, shadows the wave.
By night is a wonder weird to see,
fire on the waters. So wise lived none
of the sons of men, to search those depths!
Nay, though the heath-rover, harried by dogs,
the horn-proud hart, this holt should seek,
long distance driven, his dear life first
on the brink he yields ere he brave the plunge
to hide his head: 'tis no happy place!
Thence the welter of waters washes up
wan to welkin when winds bestir
evil storms, and air grows dusk,
and the heavens weep. Now is help once more
with thee alone! The land thou knowst not,
place of fear, where thou findest out
that sin-flecked being. Seek if thou dare!
I will reward thee, for waging this fight,
with ancient treasure, as erst I did,
with winding gold, if thou winnest back."

Chapter 20

Don't ask me that," Hrothgar replied. "More sorrows have come to us Danes. My trusted advisor Aeschere is dead. A wandering demon has taken him, and who knows where she is now, eating his flesh. She has come to avenge Grendel. I have heard tales from people who live near here. They say that there are two monsters who stalk this land, one male and one female. One of them is Grendel. Supposedly the two live in a swamp near here, a swamp where the water burns at night. No man has ever managed to explore those foul waters. Even animals would rather turn to face their hunters than go there. Evil dwells there, and now only you, Beowulf, can end it. If you dare to seek out this fiend, I will reward you tremendously."

Chapter 21

BEOWULF spake, bairn of Ecgtheow:
"Sorrow not, sage! It beseems us better
friends to avenge than fruitlessly mourn them.
Each of us all must his end abide
in the ways of the world; so win who may
glory ere death! When his days are told,
that is the warrior's worthiest doom.
Rise, O realm-warder! Ride we anon,
and mark the trail of the mother of Grendel.
No harbor shall hide her—heed my promise!—
enfolding of field or forested mountain
or floor of the flood, let her flee where she will!
But thou this day endure in patience,
as I ween thou wilt, thy woes each one."
Leaped up the graybeard: God he thanked,
mighty Lord, for the man's brave words.
For Hrothgar soon a horse was saddled
wave-maned steed. The sovran wise
stately rode on; his shield-armed men
followed in force. The footprints led
along the woodland, widely seen,
a path o'er the plain, where she passed, and trod
the murky moor; of men-at-arms
she bore the bravest and best one, dead,
him who with Hrothgar the homestead ruled.

On then went the atheling-born
o'er stone-cliffs steep and strait defiles,
narrow passes and unknown ways,
headlands sheer, and the haunts of the Nicors.
Foremost he fared, a few at his side

of the wiser men, the ways to scan,
till he found in a flash the forested hill
hanging over the hoary rock,
a woful wood: the waves below
were dyed in blood. The Danish men
had sorrow of soul, and for Scyldings all,
for many a hero, 'twas hard to bear,
ill for earls, when Aeschere's head
they found by the flood on the foreland there.
Waves were welling, the warriors saw,
hot with blood; but the horn sang oft
battle-song bold. The band sat down,
and watched on the water worm-like things,
sea-dragons strange that sounded the deep,
and nicors that lay on the ledge of the ness—
such as oft essay at hour of morn
on the road-of-sails their ruthless quest,—
and sea-snakes and monsters. These started away,
swollen and savage that song to hear,
that war-horn's blast. The warden of Geats,
with bolt from bow, then balked of life,
of wave-work, one monster, amid its heart
went the keen war-shaft; in water it seemed
less doughty in swimming whom death had seized.
Swift on the billows, with boar-spears well
hooked and barbed, it was hard beset,
done to death and dragged on the headland,
wave-roamer wondrous. Warriors viewed
the grisly guest. Then girt him Beowulf
in martial mail, nor mourned for his life.
His breastplate broad and bright of hues,
woven by hand, should the waters try;
well could it ward the warrior's body
that battle should break on his breast in vain

nor harm his heart by the hand of a foe.
And the helmet white that his head protected
was destined to dare the deeps of the flood,
through wave-whirl win: 'twas wound with chains,
decked with gold, as in days of yore
the weapon-smith worked it wondrously,
with swine-forms set it, that swords nowise,
brandished in battle, could bite that helm.
Nor was that the meanest of mighty helps
which Hrothgar's orator offered at need:
"Hrunting" they named the hilted sword,
of old-time heirlooms easily first;
iron was its edge, all etched with poison,
with battle-blood hardened, nor blenched it at fight
in hero's hand who held it ever,
on paths of peril prepared to go
to folkstead of foes. Not first time this
it was destined to do a daring task.
For he bore not in mind, the bairn of Ecglaf
sturdy and strong, that speech he had made,
drunk with wine, now this weapon he lent
to a stouter swordsman. Himself, though, durst not
under welter of waters wager his life
as loyal liegeman. So lost he his glory,
honor of earls. With the other not so,
who girded him now for the grim encounter.

Chapter 21

BEOWULF replied, "Don't despair. It is better to avenge our friends than mourn them. We're all going to die some day, so it is better for us to achieve glory before that happens. We will ride out and track down Grendel's mother. Let her run! She can't hide from us. But today, I know you will patiently endure your sorrows." Hrothgar thanked God for Beowulf's bravery and called for his horse. He took the lead, his men following closely behind. They tracked the demon's footprints through the woods and across a plain, following the path she took when she carried their friend back to her lair.

Her tracks led them along narrow cliffs, high above waters full of sea monsters. Hrothgar went in front with a few of his best trackers. Looking down, they saw that the water was full of blood. They made their way down the cliff. At the bottom they were heartbroken to discover Aeschere's head washed up on the shore. The waves were tossing and churning with blood. Monsters were everywhere in the water and on the rocky ledges. The men blew their battle horn and monsters began scurrying away and diving for cover. One briefly surfaced and the leader of the Geats shot it with an arrow. It thrashed around in the shallows, where the men speared it to death and dragged it to shore. It was an incredible sight. Beowulf prepared to enter the battle. Covered in his shining armor, unafraid of death, he got ready to dive into the murky water. His breastplate would protect him against any foe, and his helmet, covered in gold and fashioned as in the old days, would stop any sword. But the mightiest of all Beowulf's tools was the ancient, battle-tested sword that the men called "Hrunting." Unferth, afraid to fight himself, had lent the sword to the mighty warrior. The glory he lost was gained by Beowulf.

Chapter 22

BEOWULF spake, bairn of Ecgtheow:—
"Have mind, thou honored offspring of Healfdene
gold-friend of men, now I go on this quest,
sovran wise, what once was said:
if in thy cause it came that I
should lose my life, thou wouldst loyal bide
to me, though fallen, in father's place!
Be guardian, thou, to this group of my thanes,
my warrior-friends, if War should seize me;
and the goodly gifts thou gavest me,
Hrothgar beloved, to Hygelac send!
Geatland's king may ken by the gold,
Hrethel's son see, when he stares at the treasure,
that I got me a friend for goodness famed,
and joyed while I could in my jewel-bestower.
And let Unferth wield this wondrous sword,
earl far-honored, this heirloom precious,
hard of edge: with Hrunting I
seek doom of glory, or Death shall take me."

After these words the Weder-Geat lord
boldly hastened, biding never
answer at all: the ocean floods
closed o'er the hero. Long while of the day
fled ere he felt the floor of the sea.

Soon found the fiend who the flood-domain
sword-hungry held these hundred winters,
greedy and grim, that some guest from above,
some man, was raiding her monster-realm.
She grasped out for him with grisly claws,

and the warrior seized; yet scathed she not
his body hale; the breastplate hindered,
as she strove to shatter the sark of war,
the linked harness, with loathsome hand.
Then bore this brine-wolf, when bottom she touched,
the lord of rings to the lair she haunted
whiles vainly he strove, though his valor held,
weapon to wield against wondrous monsters
that sore beset him; sea-beasts many
tried with fierce tusks to tear his mail,
and swarmed on the stranger. But soon he marked
he was now in some hall, he knew not which,
where water never could work him harm,
nor through the roof could reach him ever
fangs of the flood. Firelight he saw,
beams of a blaze that brightly shone.
Then the warrior was ware of that wolf-of-the-deep,
mere-wife monstrous. For mighty stroke
he swung his blade, and the blow withheld not.
Then sang on her head that seemly blade
its war-song wild. But the warrior found
the light-of-battle was loath to bite,
to harm the heart: its hard edge failed
the noble at need, yet had known of old
strife hand to hand, and had helmets cloven,
doomed men's fighting-gear. First time, this,
for the gleaming blade that its glory fell.

Firm still stood, nor failed in valor,
heedful of high deeds, Hygelac's kinsman;
flung away fretted sword, featly jewelled,
the angry earl; on earth it lay
steel-edged and stiff. His strength he trusted,
hand-gripe of might. So man shall do

Beowulf

whenever in war he weens to earn him
lasting fame, nor fears for his life!
Seized then by shoulder, shrank not from combat,
the Geatish war-prince Grendel's mother.
Flung then the fierce one, filled with wrath,
his deadly foe, that she fell to ground.
Swift on her part she paid him back
with grisly grasp, and grappled with him.
Spent with struggle, stumbled the warrior,
fiercest of fighting-men, fell adown.
On the hall-guest she hurled herself, hent her short sword,
broad and brown-edged, the bairn to avenge,
the sole-born son.—On his shoulder lay
braided breast-mail, barring death,
withstanding entrance of edge or blade.
Life would have ended for Ecgtheow's son,
under wide earth for that earl of Geats,
had his armor of war not aided him,
battle-net hard, and holy God
wielded the victory, wisest Maker.
The Lord of Heaven allowed his cause;
and easily rose the earl erect.

Chapter 22

BEFORE he dove into the deep water, Beowulf turned to Hrothgar. "Remember what you said earlier, my lord. If I die in this battle, you will treat me as a son. Take care of my men and send the treasures you gave me to Hygelac. Let him see what a generous king you are. And give this sword back to Unferth. With Hrunting in my hand, I will achieve glory or death."

With that, Beowulf strode into the water and disappeared. It took Beowulf nearly all day to reach the bottom.

Grendel's mother soon realized that someone from the land was invading her watery lair. She reached out and grabbed Beowulf, trying to tear him apart, but his armor was too strong. She headed for her den, holding him so tightly that he could not use his sword. He saw all sorts of monsters, who kept trying to attack him. The vile beast swam to some kind of underwater hall, an area kept dry by walls and a roof. A fire burned inside. Beowulf spun free and slashed at Grendel's mother with his sword. His blade crashed against her skin but didn't penetrate. Though it was a powerful sword with a great history in battle, it could not harm this evil demon.

Beowulf tossed the sword aside. As he had done before, he would seek glory by fighting with his bare hands. He grabbed Grendel's mother by the shoulder and drove her into the ground. She jumped back to her feet and knocked Beowulf over with her powerful claw. She drew out a short sword and swung it at the hero, determined to avenge her son. The Geat's armor, however, was too strong, and the sword bent against it. He would have died if the sword had hit its mark, but God decided to spare him.

Chapter 23

MID the battle-gear saw he a blade triumphant,
old-sword of Eotens, with edge of proof,
warriors' heirloom, weapon unmatched,
—save only 'twas more than other men
to bandy-of-battle could bear at all—
as the giants had wrought it, ready and keen.
Seized then its chain-hilt the Scyldings' chieftain,
bold and battle-grim, brandished the sword,
reckless of life, and so wrathfully smote
that it gripped her neck and grasped her hard,
her bone-rings breaking: the blade pierced through
that fated-one's flesh: to floor she sank.
Bloody the blade: he was blithe of his deed.
Then blazed forth light. 'Twas bright within
as when from the sky there shines unclouded
heaven's candle. The hall he scanned.
By the wall then went he; his weapon raised
high by its hilts the Hygelac-thane,
angry and eager. That edge was not useless
to the warrior now. He wished with speed
Grendel to guerdon for grim raids many,
for the war he waged on Western-Danes
oftener far than an only time,
when of Hrothgar's hearth-companions
he slew in slumber, in sleep devoured,
fifteen men of the folk of Danes,
and as many others outward bore,
his horrible prey. Well paid for that
the wrathful prince! For now prone he saw
Grendel stretched there, spent with war,
spoiled of life, so scathed had left him

Heorot's battle. The body sprang far
when after death it endured the blow,
sword-stroke savage, that severed its head.
Soon, then, saw the sage companions
who waited with Hrothgar, watching the flood,
that the tossing waters turbid grew,
blood-stained the mere. Old men together,
hoary-haired, of the hero spake;
the warrior would not, they weened, again,
proud of conquest, come to seek
their mighty master. To many it seemed
the wolf-of-the-waves had won his life.
The ninth hour came. The noble Scyldings
left the headland; homeward went
the gold-friend of men. But the guests sat on,
stared at the surges, sick in heart,
and wished, yet weened not, their winsome lord
again to see.

Now that sword began,
from blood of the fight, in battle-droppings,
war-blade, to wane: 'twas a wondrous thing
that all of it melted as ice is wont
when frosty fetters the Father loosens,
unwinds the wave-bonds, wielding all
seasons and times: the true God he!
Nor took from that dwelling the duke of the Geats
save only the head and that hilt withal
blazoned with jewels: the blade had melted,
burned was the bright sword, her blood was so hot,
so poisoned the hell-sprite who perished within there.
Soon he was swimming who safe saw in combat
downfall of demons; up-dove through the flood.
The clashing waters were cleansed now,

waste of waves, where the wandering fiend
her life-days left and this lapsing world.
Swam then to strand the sailors'-refuge,
sturdy-in-spirit, of sea-booty glad,
of burden brave he bore with him.
Went then to greet him, and God they thanked,
the thane-band choice of their chieftain blithe,
that safe and sound they could see him again.
Soon from the hardy one helmet and armor
deftly they doffed: now drowsed the mere,
water 'neath welkin, with war-blood stained.
Forth they fared by the footpaths thence,
merry at heart the highways measured,
well-known roads. Courageous men
carried the head from the cliff by the sea,
an arduous task for all the band,
the firm in fight, since four were needed
on the shaft-of-slaughter strenuously
to bear to the gold-hall Grendel's head.
So presently to the palace there
foemen fearless, fourteen Geats,
marching came. Their master-of-clan
mighty amid them the meadow-ways trod.
Strode then within the sovran thane
fearless in fight, of fame renowned,
hardy hero, Hrothgar to greet.
And next by the hair into hall was borne
Grendel's head, where the henchmen were drinking,
an awe to clan and queen alike,
a monster of marvel: the men looked on.

Chapter 23

ARMOR and swords from previous victims were scattered around the den. Beowulf saw the sword of Eotens, said to be the greatest blade ever forged, a weapon made by and for giants. Ordinary men couldn't even lift it. Beowulf snatched it up and swung wildly, catching Grendel's mother across the neck. It cut through her skin and shattered her bones. She collapsed on the floor, doomed. Beowulf was happy with his bloody work. Suddenly, the hall filled with light. Beowulf looked around and saw that Grendel's body was resting there. He decided to take revenge for all the men Grendel had killed. He strode up to the body and, using his new sword, severed the monster's head. Meanwhile, the men on shore saw that the waters were running with blood. Some said that Beowulf must be dead. It had been nine hours and they were growing sure that Grendel's mother must have won the battle. Some of them, including Hrothgar, began to make their way home. The Geats, however, waited for their leader to return from the bloody deep.

Down below, the blood of the monsters caused the great sword to melt like ice that's been heated. This showed God's great power. Though the monster's den was full of treasure, Beowulf decided to take only Grendel's head and the jewel-covered hilt of the now-melted sword. He swam for the surface. The water was growing lighter as the evil influence of Grendel's mother wore off. Beowulf surfaced and made his way to the shore. His men were overjoyed to see him and thanked God for saving their brave leader. They helped Beowulf pull off his armor, and they started back on the footpaths they had taken from Heorot. Grendel's head was so heavy that it took four of them to carry it. They all marched together, with Beowulf in the middle. They strode into the hall, dragging Grendel's head by the hair. The people inside, including the queen, were eating and drinking, and they looked up in astonishment.

Chapter 24

B EOWULF spake, bairn of Ecgtheow:—
"Lo, now, this sea-booty, son of Healfdene,
Lord of Scyldings, we've lustily brought thee,
sign of glory; thou seest it here.
Not lightly did I with my life escape!
In war under water this work I essayed
with endless effort; and even so
my strength had been lost had the Lord not shielded me.
Not a whit could I with Hrunting do
in work of war, though the weapon is good;
yet a sword the Sovran of Men vouchsafed me
to spy on the wall there, in splendor hanging,
old, gigantic,—how oft He guides
the friendless wight!—and I fought with that brand,
felling in fight, since fate was with me,
the house's wardens. That war-sword then
all burned, bright blade, when the blood gushed o'er it,
battle-sweat hot; but the hilt I brought back
from my foes. So avenged I their fiendish deeds
death-fall of Danes, as was due and right.
And this is my hest, that in Heorot now
safe thou canst sleep with thy soldier band,
and every thane of all thy folk
both old and young; no evil fear,
Scyldings' lord, from that side again,
aught ill for thy earls, as erst thou must!"
Then the golden hilt, for that gray-haired leader,
hoary hero, in hand was laid,
giant-wrought, old. So owned and enjoyed it
after downfall of devils, the Danish lord,
wonder-smiths' work, since the world was rid

of that grim-souled fiend, the foe of God,
murder-marked, and his mother as well.
Now it passed into power of the people's king,
best of all that the oceans bound
who have scattered their gold o'er Scandia's isle.
Hrothgar spake—the hilt he viewed,
heirloom old, where was etched the rise
of that far-off fight when the floods o'erwhelmed,
raging waves, the race of giants
(fearful their fate!), a folk estranged
from God Eternal: whence guerdon due
in that waste of waters the Wielder paid them.
So on the guard of shining gold
in runic staves it was rightly said
for whom the serpent-traced sword was wrought,
best of blades, in bygone days,
and the hilt well wound.—The wise-one spake,
son of Healfdene; silent were all:—
"Lo, so may he say who sooth and right
follows 'mid folk, of far times mindful,
a land-warden old, that this earl belongs
to the better breed! So, borne aloft,
thy fame must fly, O friend my Beowulf,
far and wide o'er folksteads many. Firmly thou
shalt all maintain,
mighty strength with mood of wisdom. Love of
mine will I assure thee,
as, awhile ago, I promised; thou shalt prove a stay
in future,
in far-off years, to folk of thine,
to the heroes a help. Was not Heremod thus
to offspring of Ecgwela, Honor-Scyldings,
nor grew for their grace, but for grisly slaughter,
for doom of death to the Danishmen.

* * *

He slew, wrath-swollen, his shoulder-comrades,
companions at board! So he passed alone,
chieftain haughty, from human cheer.
Though him the Maker with might endowed,
delights of power, and uplifted high
above all men, yet blood-fierce his mind,
his breast-hoard, grew, no bracelets gave he
to Danes as was due; he endured all joyless
strain of struggle and stress of woe,
long feud with his folk. Here find thy lesson!
Of virtue advise thee! This verse I have said for thee,
wise from lapsed winters. Wondrous seems
how to sons of men Almighty God
in the strength of His spirit sendeth wisdom,
estate, high station: He swayeth all things.
Whiles He letteth right lustily fare
the heart of the hero of high-born race,—
in seat ancestral assigns him bliss,
his folk's sure fortress in fee to hold,
puts in his power great parts of the earth,
empire so ample, that end of it
this wanter-of-wisdom weeneth none.
So he waxes in wealth, nowise can harm him
illness or age; no evil cares
shadow his spirit; no sword-hate threatens
from ever an enemy: all the world
wends at his will, no worse he knoweth,
till all within him obstinate pride
waxes and wakes while the warden slumbers,
the spirit's sentry; sleep is too fast
which masters his might, and the murderer nears,
stealthily shooting the shafts from his bow!

Chapter 24

"HROTHGAR," Beowulf called out, "we have brought you this treasure from the sea. I nearly lost my life getting it. I fought hard and would have lost my strength if God hadn't protected me. Hrunting is a good sword, but it completely failed me. Thankfully, God showed me another sword hanging on the wall, an old sword of the giants. I used it to kill the beasts that lived in that foul den. Their blood melted the blade, but I brought the hilt back. I've avenged the deaths of the Danes. Everyone in Heorot can sleep safely now." Beowulf handed the golden hilt to Hrothgar. That gift became the most treasured possession of the Danish princes, a sign of the evils that once plagued them. Hrothgar examined the hilt, looking carefully at the ancient etchings on it. They told the story of how war was born and the giants were cut off from the Lord, who flooded the world. Everyone was quiet as Hrothgar studied the hilt. He looked up and spoke, "Beowulf, you were born for glory. Your name is known everywhere. You combine great strength with wisdom. I repeat my promise of friendship, and I know that you will be a great gift to your people for years to come. Our former king Heremod was different. He brought suffering to his people.

"Heremod was bloodthirsty and violent. Learn a lesson from this. Seek virtue. I am old enough to know how true this is. God is mysterious. He hands out wisdom and power to men, and some men use their gifts so much that they forget that they are mortal. They forget that God has blessed them. Such a man does not care about this world or his enemies. He thinks nothing can harm him and that the world must bend to his will. Eventually he grows too proud. When this happens, it is as though he has been shot in the heart by a demon."

Chapter 25

UNDER harness his heart then is hit indeed
by sharpest shafts; and no shelter avails
from foul behest of the hellish fiend.
Him seems too little what long he possessed.
Greedy and grim, no golden rings
he gives for his pride; the promised future
forgets he and spurns, with all God has sent him,
Wonder-Wielder, of wealth and fame.
Yet in the end it ever comes
that the frame of the body fragile yields,
fated falls; and there follows another
who joyously the jewels divides,
the royal riches, nor recks of his forebear.
Ban, then, such baleful thoughts, Beowulf dearest,
best of men, and the better part choose,
profit eternal; and temper thy pride,
warrior famous! The flower of thy might
lasts now a while: but erelong it shall be
that sickness or sword thy strength shall minish,
or fang of fire, or flooding billow,
or bite of blade, or brandished spear,
or odious age; or the eyes' clear beam
wax dull and darken: Death even thee
in haste shall o'erwhelm, thou hero of war!
So the Ring-Danes these half-years a hundred I ruled,
wielded 'neath welkin, and warded them bravely
from mighty-ones many o'er middle-earth,
from spear and sword, till it seemed for me
no foe could be found under fold of the sky.
Lo, sudden the shift! To me seated secure
came grief for joy when Grendel began
to harry my home, the hellish foe;

for those ruthless raids, unresting I suffered
heart-sorrow heavy. Heaven be thanked,
Lord Eternal, for life extended
that I on this head all hewn and bloody,
after long evil, with eyes may gaze!
—Go to the bench now! Be glad at banquet,
warrior worthy! A wealth of treasure
at dawn of day, be dealt between us!"

Glad was the Geats' lord, going betimes
to seek his seat, as the Sage commanded.
Afresh, as before, for the famed-in-battle,
for the band of the hall, was a banquet dight
nobly anew. The Night-Helm darkened
dusk o'er the drinkers.
The doughty ones rose:
for the hoary-headed would hasten to rest,
aged Scylding; and eager the Geat,
shield-fighter sturdy, for sleeping yearned.
Him wander-weary, warrior-guest
from far, a hall-thane heralded forth,
who by custom courtly cared for all
needs of a thane as in those old days
warrior-wanderers wont to have.
So slumbered the stout-heart. Stately the hall
rose gabled and gilt where the guest slept on
till a raven black the rapture-of-heaven
blithe-heart boded. Bright came flying
shine after shadow. The swordsmen hastened,
athelings all were eager homeward
forth to fare; and far from thence
the great-hearted guest would guide his keel.

* * *

Bade then the hardy-one Hrunting be brought
to the son of Ecglaf, the sword bade him take,
excellent iron, and uttered his thanks for it,
quoth that he counted it keen in battle,
"war-friend" winsome: with words he slandered not
edge of the blade: 'twas a big-hearted man!
Now eager for parting and armed at point
warriors waited, while went to his host
that Darling of Danes. The doughty atheling
to high-seat hastened and Hrothgar greeted.

Chapter 25

ONCE his heart is struck by the demon's arrow, he becomes greedy. He forgets the customs of his ancestors and ignores warning signs about his coming doom. But eventually he dies and all of the wealth he had is spread out among other people. Avoid becoming a man like that, Beowulf. Keep your pride in check. Now you are strong, but sooner or later your strength will begin to fail you, and time or the sword will make it clear that you are mortal. Death will come even for you. I've ruled the Danes for half a century and protected them from every evil. It began to seem that there was nothing in the world that could get past me. But everything changed so fast. My sense of security disappeared when Grendel first entered this hall. Thank God that I can now look upon his severed head! Please, Beowulf—sit and feast! Tomorrow you will receive much treasure."

Beowulf happily sat down, and soon the feast resumed. Everyone was in a good mood as night descended upon the land. Eventually Hrothgar and Beowulf both rose to go to bed. One of the hall guards showed Beowulf to his sleeping quarters. The brave-hearted warrior slept. The hall stood peacefully in the darkness. Beowulf slept until the raven called in the morning. Men were up and about, eager to get home.

Beowulf gave Hrunting back to Unferth, thanking him for it. Even though he had found a better sword, he didn't say anything bad about Hrunting, because he was a good man. With his warriors waiting and eager to leave, Beowulf went to Hrothgar.

Chapter 26

BEOWULF spake, bairn of Ecgtheow:—
"Lo, we seafarers say our will,
far-come men, that we fain would seek
Hygelac now. We here have found
hosts to our heart: thou hast harbored us well.
If ever on earth I am able to win me
more of thy love, O lord of men,
aught anew, than I now have done,
for work of war I am willing still!
If it come to me ever across the seas
that neighbor foemen annoy and fright thee,—
as they that hate thee erewhile have used,—
thousands then of thanes I shall bring,
heroes to help thee. Of Hygelac I know,
ward of his folk, that, though few his years,
the lord of the Geats will give me aid
by word and by work, that well I may serve thee,
wielding the war-wood to win thy triumph
and lending thee might when thou lackest men.
If thy Hrethric should come to court of Geats,
a sovran's son, he will surely there
find his friends. A far-off land
each man should visit who vaunts him brave."

Him then answering, Hrothgar spake:—
"These words of thine the wisest God
sent to thy soul! No sager counsel
from so young in years e'er yet have I heard.
Thou art strong of main and in mind art wary,
art wise in words! I ween indeed
if ever it hap that Hrethel's heir
by spear be seized, by sword-grim battle,

Beowulf

by illness or iron, thine elder and lord,
people's leader,—and life be thine,—
no seemlier man will the Sea-Geats find
at all to choose for their chief and king,
for hoard-guard of heroes, if hold thou wilt
thy kinsman's kingdom! Thy keen mind pleases me
the longer the better, Beowulf loved!

Thou hast brought it about that both our peoples,
sons of the Geat and Spear-Dane folk,
shall have mutual peace, and from murderous strife,
such as once they waged, from war refrain.
Long as I rule this realm so wide,
let our hoards be common, let heroes with gold
each other greet o'er the gannet's-bath,
and the ringed-prow bear o'er rolling waves
tokens of love. I trow my landfolk
towards friend and foe are firmly joined,
and honor they keep in the olden way."

To him in the hall, then, Healfdene's son
gave treasures twelve, and the trust-of-earls
bade him fare with the gifts to his folk beloved,
hale to his home, and in haste return.
Then kissed the king of kin renowned,
Scyldings' chieftain, that choicest thane,
and fell on his neck. Fast flowed the tears
of the hoary-headed. Heavy with winters,
he had chances twain, but he clung to this,—
that each should look on the other again,
and hear him in hall. Was this hero so dear to him.
his breast's wild billows he banned in vain;
safe in his soul a secret longing,
locked in his mind, for that loved man

burned in his blood. Then Beowulf strode,
glad of his gold-gifts, the grass-plot o'er,
warrior blithe. The wave-roamer bode
riding at anchor, its owner awaiting.
As they hastened onward, Hrothgar's gift
they lauded at length.—'Twas a lord unpeered,
every way blameless, till age had broken
—it spareth no mortal—his splendid might.

Chapter 26

BEOWULF said to Hrothgar, "We plan to return to our homeland now. You have been wonderful hosts, and we hold you dear to our hearts. If there is ever anything else I can do for you, I am ready. If ever you are troubled with war, I will cross the sea with thousands of warriors to fight by your side. Hygelac is young, but I have faith that he will support me if ever you need our assistance. If your son Hrethric comes to Geatland, he will be among friends. Any land is happy to welcome a brave man."

Hrothgar replied, "The wisdom of your words must be a gift from God. I've never heard such thoughts from someone so young. You are strong in body and in mind. If ever your king should fall in battle or through sickness, the Geats will not find a better leader than you, if you would be willing to be their protector. Your mind pleases me the more I'm with you, dear Beowulf!

"You have made sure that the Geats and the Spear-Danes will be close friends. As long as I am king, our treasures will be shared, our warriors will greet each other happily, and we will send signs of our love across the seas. Our people will keep to the true old customs."

Then Hrothgar gave Beowulf twelve treasures and told him to be safe in his journey home and to return soon. In tears, Hrothgar embraced Beowulf. The old man couldn't shake the feeling that they would never see each other again, and Beowulf was so dear to him that this fear brought the king to tears. Beowulf strode to his ship and he and his men departed. On the journey, they praised Hrothgar's goodness repeatedly. He would be a great king until time defeated him, as it always does.

Chapter 27

CAME now to ocean the ever-courageous
hardy henchmen, their harness bearing,
woven war-sarks. The warden marked,
trusty as ever, the earl's return.
From the height of the hill no hostile words
reached the guests as he rode to greet them;
but "Welcome!" he called to that Weder clan
as the sheen-mailed spoilers to ship marched on.
Then on the strand, with steeds and treasure
and armor their roomy and ring-dight ship
was heavily laden: high its mast
rose over Hrothgar's hoarded gems.
A sword to the boat-guard Beowulf gave,
mounted with gold; on the mead-bench since
he was better esteemed, that blade possessing,
heirloom old.—Their ocean-keel boarding,
they drove through the deep, and Daneland left.
A sea-cloth was set, a sail with ropes,
firm to the mast; the flood-timbers moaned;
nor did wind over billows that wave-swimmer blow
across from her course. The craft sped on,
foam-necked it floated forth o'er the waves,
keel firm-bound over briny currents,
till they got them sight of the Geatish cliffs,
home-known headlands. High the boat,
stirred by winds, on the strand updrove.
Helpful at haven the harbor-guard stood,
who long already for loved companions
by the water had waited and watched afar.
He bound to the beach the broad-bosomed ship
with anchor-bands, lest ocean-billows
that trusty timber should tear away.

Then Beowulf bade them bear the treasure,
gold and jewels; no journey far
was it thence to go to the giver of rings,
Hygelac Hrethling: at home he dwelt
by the sea-wall close, himself and clan.
Haughty that house, a hero the king,
high the hall, and Hygd right young,
wise and wary, though winters few
in those fortress walls she had found a home,
Haereth's daughter. Nor humble her ways,
nor grudged she gifts to the Geatish men,
of precious treasure. Not Thryth's pride showed she,
folk-queen famed, or that fell deceit.
Was none so daring that durst make bold
(save her lord alone) of the liegemen dear
that lady full in the face to look,
but forged fetters he found his lot,
bonds of death! And brief the respite;
soon as they seized him, his sword-doom was spoken,
and the burnished blade a baleful murder
proclaimed and closed. No queenly way
for woman to practise, though peerless she,
that the weaver-of-peace from warrior dear
by wrath and lying his life should reave!
But Hemming's kinsman hindered this.—

For over their ale men also told
that of these folk-horrors fewer she wrought,
onslaughts of evil, after she went,
gold-decked bride, to the brave young prince,
atheling haughty, and Offa's hall
o'er the fallow flood at her father's bidding
safely sought, where since she prospered,
royal, throned, rich in goods,

fain of the fair life fate had sent her,
and leal in love to the lord of warriors.
He, of all heroes I heard of ever
from sea to sea, of the sons of earth,
most excellent seemed. Hence Offa was praised
for his fighting and feeing by far-off men,
the spear-bold warrior; wisely he ruled
over his empire. Eomer woke to him,
help of heroes, Hemming's kinsman,
Grandson of Garmund, grim in war.

Chapter 27

THE Geats passed by the guard at the shore. He called out a greeting to them as they loaded their treasure aboard the ship. Beowulf gave a jeweled sword to the man who guarded the boat. This gift earned the man much respect in the beer hall. The Geats headed out into the ocean, leaving Denmark behind. They sailed straight on to Geatland and soon were in sight of their homeland. The Geats' coast guard had been waiting and watching for them. The guard anchored the ship to the shore so that the winds wouldn't carry it away. Beowulf and his men unloaded the treasure. They were taking it to Hygelac's home, which was not far from the shore. The house was a grand one, fit for a heroic king. Hygelac lived there with his wife, Hygd, who was young for a queen but thoughtful and generous. She was the opposite of Queen Modthyrth of old, who would have any man killed who dared to look her in the face. That is not how a queen should behave, even if she is beautiful.

But, as the legend goes, Modthyrth was not as cruel after she was married to the great prince Offa. He was one of the mightiest warriors of all.

Chapter 28

HASTENED the hardy one, henchmen with him,
sandy strand of the sea to tread
and widespread ways. The world's great candle,
sun shone from south. They strode along
with sturdy steps to the spot they knew
where the battle-king young, his burg within,
slayer of Ongentheow, shared the rings,
shelter-of-heroes. To Hygelac
Beowulf's coming was quickly told,—
that there in the court the clansmen's refuge,
the shield-companion sound and alive,
hale from the hero-play homeward strode.
With haste in the hall, by highest order,
room for the rovers was readily made.
By his sovran he sat, come safe from battle,
kinsman by kinsman. His kindly lord
he first had greeted in gracious form,
with manly words. The mead dispensing,
came through the high hall Haereth's daughter,
winsome to warriors, wine-cup bore
to the hands of the heroes. Hygelac then
his comrade fairly with question plied
in the lofty hall, sore longing to know
what manner of sojourn the Sea-Geats made.
"What came of thy quest, my kinsman Beowulf,
when thy yearnings suddenly swept thee yonder
battle to seek o'er the briny sea,
combat in Heorot? Hrothgar couldst thou
aid at all, the honored chief,
in his wide-known woes? With waves of care
my sad heart seethed; I sore mistrusted
my loved one's venture: long I begged thee

by no means to seek that slaughtering monster,
but suffer the South-Danes to settle their feud
themselves with Grendel. Now God be thanked
that safe and sound I can see thee now!"

Beowulf spake, the bairn of Ecgtheow:—
"'Tis known and unhidden, Hygelac Lord,
to many men, that meeting of ours,
struggle grim between Grendel and me,
which we fought on the field where full too many
sorrows he wrought for the Scylding-Victors,
evils unending. These all I avenged.
No boast can be from breed of Grendel,
any on earth, for that uproar at dawn,
from the longest-lived of the loathsome race
in fleshly fold!—But first I went
Hrothgar to greet in the hall of gifts,
where Healfdene's kinsman high-renowned,
soon as my purpose was plain to him,
assigned me a seat by his son and heir.
The liegemen were lusty; my life-days never
such merry men over mead in hall
have I heard under heaven! The high-born queen,
people's peace-bringer, passed through the hall,
cheered the young clansmen, clasps of gold,
ere she sought her seat, to sundry gave.
Oft to the heroes Hrothgar's daughter,
to earls in turn, the ale-cup tendered,—
she whom I heard these hall-companions
Freawaru name, when fretted gold
she proffered the warriors. Promised is she,
gold-decked maid, to the glad son of Froda.
Sage this seems to the Scylding's-friend,
kingdom's-keeper: he counts it wise

the woman to wed so and ward off feud,
store of slaughter. But seldom ever
when men are slain, does the murder-spear sink
but briefest while, though the bride be fair!

"Nor haply will like it the Heathobard lord,
and as little each of his liegemen all,
when a thane of the Danes, in that doughty throng,
goes with the lady along their hall,
and on him the old-time heirlooms glisten
hard and ring-decked, Heathobard's treasure,
weapons that once they wielded fair
until they lost at the linden-play
liegeman leal and their lives as well.
Then, over the ale, on this heirloom gazing,
some ash-wielder old who has all in mind
that spear-death of men,—he is stern of mood,
heavy at heart,—in the hero young
tests the temper and tries the soul
and war-hate wakens, with words like these:—
Canst thou not, comrade, ken that sword
which to the fray thy father carried
in his final feud, 'neath the fighting-mask,
dearest of blades, when the Danish slew him
and wielded the war-place on Withergild's fall,
after havoc of heroes, those hardy Scyldings?
Now, the son of a certain slaughtering Dane,
proud of his treasure, paces this hall,
joys in the killing, and carries the jewel
that rightfully ought to be owned by thee!
Thus he urges and eggs him all the time
with keenest words, till occasion offers
that Freawaru's thane, for his father's deed,
after bite of brand in his blood must slumber,

losing his life; but that liegeman flies
living away, for the land he kens.
And thus be broken on both their sides
oaths of the earls, when Ingeld's breast
wells with war-hate, and wife-love now
after the care-billows cooler grows.
So I hold not high the Heathobards' faith
due to the Danes, or their during love
and pact of peace.—But I pass from that,
turning to Grendel, O giver-of-treasure,
and saying in full how the fight resulted,
hand-fray of heroes. When heaven's jewel
had fled o'er far fields, that fierce sprite came,
night-foe savage, to seek us out
where safe and sound we sentried the hall.
To Hondscio then was that harassing deadly,
his fall there was fated. He first was slain,
girded warrior. Grendel on him
turned murderous mouth, on our mighty kinsman,
and all of the brave man's body devoured.
Yet none the earlier, empty-handed,
would the bloody-toothed murderer, mindful of bale,
outward go from the gold-decked hall:
but me he attacked in his terror of might,
with greedy hand grasped me. A glove hung by him
wide and wondrous, wound with bands;
and in artful wise it all was wrought,
by devilish craft, of dragon-skins.
Me therein, an innocent man,
the fiendish foe was fain to thrust
with many another. He might not so,
when I all angrily upright stood.
'Twere long to relate how that land-destroyer
I paid in kind for his cruel deeds;

yet there, my prince, this people of thine
got fame by my fighting. He fled away,
and a little space his life preserved;
but there staid behind him his stronger hand
left in Heorot; heartsick thence
on the floor of the ocean that outcast fell.
Me for this struggle the Scyldings'-friend
paid in plenty with plates of gold,
with many a treasure, when morn had come
and we all at the banquet-board sat down.
Then was song and glee. The gray-haired Scylding,
much tested, told of the times of yore.
Whiles the hero his harp bestirred,
wood-of-delight; now lays he chanted
of sooth and sadness, or said aright
legends of wonder, the wide-hearted king;
or for years of his youth he would yearn at times,
for strength of old struggles, now stricken with age,
hoary hero: his heart surged full
when, wise with winters, he wailed their flight.
Thus in the hall the whole of that day
at ease we feasted, till fell o'er earth
another night. Anon full ready
in greed of vengeance, Grendel's mother
set forth all doleful. Dead was her son
through war-hate of Weders; now, woman monstrous
with fury fell a foeman she slew,
avenged her offspring. From Aeschere old,
loyal councillor, life was gone;
nor might they e'en, when morning broke,
those Danish people, their death-done comrade
burn with brands, on balefire lay
the man they mourned. Under mountain stream
she had carried the corpse with cruel hands.

Beowulf

For Hrothgar that was the heaviest sorrow
of all that had laden the lord of his folk.
The leader then, by thy life, besought me
(sad was his soul) in the sea-waves' coil
to play the hero and hazard my being
for glory of prowess: my guerdon he pledged.
I then in the waters—'tis widely known—
that sea-floor-guardian savage found.
Hand-to-hand there a while we struggled;
billows welled blood; in the briny hall
her head I hewed with a hardy blade
from Grendel's mother,—and gained my life,
though not without danger. My doom was not yet.
Then the haven-of-heroes, Healfdene's son,
gave me in guerdon great gifts of price.

Chapter 28

BEOWULF hurried to the hall. Hygelac soon heard of the return of the hero and ordered that the hall be made ready to welcome him. Hygelac greeted his loyal warrior and the two men sat down together. The king wanted to know all about Beowulf's adventure. "How did it all turn out, Beowulf? You left here so quickly, hurrying to help destroy the evil that plagued Heorot. Were you successful? Did you help Hrothgar? I was heartsick at your absence. I didn't want you to go after that slaughtering monster. I wanted you to let the Danes take care of Grendel themselves. Thank God you are safe and back home!"

Beowulf replied, "The battle I had with Grendel is now well known among many men. I fought him in the very hall where he had caused so much suffering, and I avenged all those who died. No descendents of Grendel, no matter how long they may live, will brag about what happened there. But the first thing I did was greet Hrothgar and tell him why I had come. He asked me to sit next to his son at the table. The men in the hall were very happy, and I've never seen such great drinkers! The queen came into the hall and lifted the spirits of all the men. Freawaru, Hrothgar's daughter, was there as well, handing around the ale cup. She is supposed to be married to Froda's son. That union will hopefully help his people, the Heathobards, and the Danes put aside their old feud. But even the most beautiful bride cannot stop the spears if violence arises.

"Think about it: When the Danes and Heathobards are together at the wedding feast, someone will no doubt remember the old fighting. The Heathobards will see the treasure that the Danes took from them the last time they battled, and one of them—most likely an old man who remembers the past well—will urge them to renew their feud.

And then all of their promises of friendship will be worth nothing. I don't hold much hope for lasting peace between the Heathobards and the Danes. But enough of that. When the sun had set, Grendel came to the hall to attack us. The monster killed Hondscio and ate him. But that was the only man he got, because the next one he tried to attack was me. He carried a strange pouch made of dragon skin, and he tried to stuff me in there. I sprung free before he could get me. It would take a long time to tell you every detail of the fight, but with that battle I earned glory for your people. Grendel ran away, but his arm stayed behind in Heorot, where I tore it off. He died at the bottom of his swamp. The next morning the Scyldings gave me a lot of treasure as a reward for my victory. There was a banquet with a lot of music and good cheer. The king and other old men entertained everyone with tales about the ancient days. We feasted that way for the entire day. That night, however, Grendel's mother came to seek revenge for her son. She killed Aeschere, Hrothgar's closest advisor, and took him back to her lair. That was the worst blow to Hrothgar, who then asked me to go kill the she-wolf who took his friend. So, as many men already know, I dove into the water where she lived. We fought for a long time down there, and the waves were full of blood. I found a sword in her lair that I used to cut off her head. Hrothgar gave me many gifts for this feat. Hrothgar kept his word and practiced the old customs. He gave me many gifts, all of which I am happy to offer to you, my lord. I have so few kinsmen except for you, Hygelac."

Chapter 29

So held this king to the customs old,
that I wanted for nought in the wage I gained,
the meed of my might; he made me gifts,
Healfdene's heir, for my own disposal.
Now to thee, my prince, I proffer them all,
gladly give them. Thy grace alone
can find me favor. Few indeed
have I of kinsmen, save, Hygelac, thee!"
Then he bade them bear him the boar-head standard,
the battle-helm high, and breastplate gray,
the splendid sword; then spake in form:—
"Me this war-gear the wise old prince,
Hrothgar, gave, and his hest he added,
that its story be straightway said to thee.—
A while it was held by Heorogar king,
for long time lord of the land of Scyldings;
yet not to his son the sovran left it,
to daring Heoroweard,—dear as he was to him,
his harness of battle.—Well hold thou it all!"

And I heard that soon passed o'er the path of this treasure,
all apple-fallow, four good steeds,
each like the others, arms and horses
he gave to the king. So should kinsmen be,
not weave one another the net of wiles,
or with deep-hid treachery death contrive
for neighbor and comrade. His nephew was ever
by hardy Hygelac held full dear,
and each kept watch o'er the other's weal.
I heard, too, the necklace to Hygd he presented,
wonder-wrought treasure, which Wealtheow gave him
sovran's daughter: three steeds he added,

slender and saddle-gay. Since such gift
the gem gleamed bright on the breast of the queen.

Thus showed his strain the son of Ecgtheow
as a man remarked for mighty deeds
and acts of honor. At ale he slew not
comrade or kin; nor cruel his mood,
though of sons of earth his strength was greatest,
a glorious gift that God had sent
the splendid leader. Long was he spurned,
and worthless by Geatish warriors held;
him at mead the master-of-clans
failed full oft to favor at all.
Slack and shiftless the strong men deemed him,
profitless prince; but payment came,
to the warrior honored, for all his woes.—

Then the bulwark-of-earls bade bring within,
hardy chieftain, Hrethel's heirloom
garnished with gold: no Geat e'er knew
in shape of a sword a statelier prize.
The brand he laid in Beowulf's lap;
and of hides assigned him seven thousand,
with house and high-seat. They held in common
land alike by their line of birth,
inheritance, home: but higher the king
because of his rule o'er the realm itself.

Now further it fell with the flight of years,
with harryings horrid, that Hygelac perished,
and Heardred, too, by hewing of swords
under the shield-wall slaughtered lay,
when him at the van of his victor-folk
sought hardy heroes, Heatho-Scilfings,

Beowulf

in arms o'erwhelming Hereric's nephew.
Then Beowulf came as king this broad
realm to wield; and he ruled it well
fifty winters, a wise old prince,
warding his land, until One began
in the dark of night, a Dragon, to rage.
In the grave on the hill a hoard it guarded,
in the stone-barrow steep. A strait path reached it,
unknown to mortals. Some man, however,
came by chance that cave within
to the heathen hoard. In hand he took
a golden goblet, nor gave he it back,
stole with it away, while the watcher slept,
by thievish wiles: for the warden's wrath
prince and people must pay betimes!

Chapter 29

BEOWULF had his men bring forward the splendid weapons and armor he got from Hrothgar. "Hrothgar gave me all of this," Beowulf said, "and he asked me to tell you that it used to belong to his brother Heorogar, king of the Scyldings. Heorogar did not give it to his son, even though that man, Heoroweard, was quite brave. And now it is yours to enjoy!"

Beowulf also gave four armored horses to his king. This is how kinsmen should behave to each other. They shouldn't plot against one another and try to do harm. Hygelac was Beowulf's uncle, and the two men looked out for each other. Beowulf also gave Hygd, Hygelac's wife, the beautiful necklace he had received from Wealtheow, along with three horses. That necklace shined brightly on the queen's breast.

By doing these things, Beowulf showed that he was not only brave, but honorable, as well. He did not attack drunk men, and he was never cruel, even though God had blessed him with greater strength than any man. Some of the Geats had looked down on Beowulf in times past, believing him to be weak and lazy. He proved them wrong.

King Hygelac asked for the most glorious sword of the Geats, Hrethel's old blade, to be brought in and placed in Beowulf's lap. He also gave Beowulf a huge swath of land, along with a grand house.

In later years, Hygelac was killed in battle, and Heardred, his heir, was unable to protect the people and was slaughtered in battle. So Beowulf became their king. For fifty years, he was a wise and good ruler. But then evil came to Beowulf's land in the form of a dragon. The dragon had a vast treasure in its lair in the mountains. Somehow a man found his way into the lair and stole a goblet while the dragon was sleeping. For this crime, the people would all suffer.

Chapter 30

THAT way he went with no will of his own,
in danger of life, to the dragon's hoard,
but for pressure of peril, some prince's thane.
He fled in fear the fatal scourge,
seeking shelter, a sinful man,
and entered in. At the awful sight
tottered that guest, and terror seized him;
yet the wretched fugitive rallied anon
from fright and fear ere he fled away,
and took the cup from that treasure-hoard.
Of such besides there was store enough,
heirlooms old, the earth below,
which some earl forgotten, in ancient years,
left the last of his lofty race,
heedfully there had hidden away,
dearest treasure. For death of yore
had hurried all hence; and he alone
left to live, the last of the clan,
weeping his friends, yet wished to bide
warding the treasure, his one delight,
though brief his respite. The barrow, new-ready,
to strand and sea-waves stood anear,
hard by the headland, hidden and closed;
there laid within it his lordly heirlooms
and heaped hoard of heavy gold
that warden of rings. Few words he spake:

"Now hold thou, earth, since heroes may not,
what earls have owned! Lo, erst from thee
brave men brought it! But battle-death seized
and cruel killing my clansmen all,
robbed them of life and a liegeman's joys.

Beowulf

None have I left to lift the sword,
or to cleanse the carven cup of price,
beaker bright. My brave are gone.
And the helmet hard, all haughty with gold,
shall part from its plating. Polishers sleep
who could brighten and burnish the battle-mask;
and those weeds of war that were wont to brave
over bicker of shields the bite of steel
rust with their bearer. The ringed mail
fares not far with famous chieftain,
at side of hero! No harp's delight,
no glee-wood's gladness! No good hawk now
flies through the hall! Nor horses fleet
stamp in the burgstead! Battle and death
the flower of my race have reft away."
Mournful of mood, thus he moaned his woe,
alone, for them all, and unblithe wept
by day and by night, till death's fell wave
o'erwhelmed his heart. His hoard-of-bliss
that old ill-doer open found,
who, blazing at twilight the barrows haunteth,
naked foe-dragon flying by night
folded in fire: the folk of earth
dread him sore. 'Tis his doom to seek
hoard in the graves, and heathen gold
to watch, many-wintered: nor wins he thereby!

Powerful this plague-of-the-people thus
held the house of the hoard in earth
three hundred winters; till One aroused
wrath in his breast, to the ruler bearing
that costly cup, and the king implored
for bond of peace. So the barrow was plundered,
borne off was booty. His boon was granted

that wretched man; and his ruler saw
first time what was fashioned in far-off days.

When the dragon awoke, new woe was kindled.
O'er the stone he snuffed. The stark-heart found
footprint of foe who so far had gone
in his hidden craft by the creature's head.—
So may the undoomed easily flee
evils and exile, if only he gain
the grace of The Wielder!—That warden of gold
o'er the ground went seeking, greedy to find
the man who wrought him such wrong in sleep.
Savage and burning, the barrow he circled
all without; nor was any there,
none in the waste. . . . Yet war he desired,
was eager for battle. The barrow he entered,
sought the cup, and discovered soon
that some one of mortals had searched his treasure,
his lordly gold. The guardian waited
ill-enduring till evening came;
boiling with wrath was the barrow's keeper,
and fain with flame the foe to pay
for the dear cup's loss.—Now day was fled
as the worm had wished. By its wall no more
was it glad to bide, but burning flew
folded in flame: a fearful beginning
for sons of the soil; and soon it came,
in the doom of their lord, to a dreadful end.

Chapter 30

THE thief had not gone to the dragon's lair on purpose, and he didn't mean to steal the goblet. He was a slave who had run away from his cruel master and used the den as a hiding place. He was examining the treasure when the dragon appeared, and it scared him so much that he ran out while still holding the goblet. The vast treasure had been left there by an ancient lord. He was the last of his race, and after all his companions died, he had only his treasure to keep him company.

He asked the earth to hold the treasure that he could not, since death would loosen his grip on his gold. No one wore the armor buried there, and no one picked up the swords. War and death took them all. The lord mourned day and night until death finally took him as well.

The dragon, which was cursed to guard the treasure left in graves, found the hoard. It stayed there for three hundred years before the old runaway slave stumbled in. He took the goblet back to his master, hoping to win his master's favor, and the master and his men returned to take as much of the treasure as they could.

When the dragon woke up, it saw the footprints leading through its lair. It began searching for the thief, attacking and burning everything in his sight. The people suffered, though soon enough their king would suffer, as well.

Chapter 31

THEN the baleful fiend its fire belched out,
and bright homes burned. The blaze stood high
all landsfolk frighting. No living thing
would that loathly one leave as aloft it flew.
Wide was the dragon's warring seen,
its fiendish fury far and near,
as the grim destroyer those Geatish people
hated and hounded. To hidden lair,
to its hoard it hastened at hint of dawn.
Folk of the land it had lapped in flame,
with bale and brand. In its barrow it trusted,
its battling and bulwarks: that boast was vain!

To Beowulf then the bale was told
quickly and truly: the king's own home,
of buildings the best, in brand-waves melted,
that gift-throne of Geats. To the good old man
sad in heart, 'twas heaviest sorrow.
The sage assumed that his sovran God
he had angered, breaking ancient law,
and embittered the Lord. His breast within
with black thoughts welled, as his wont was never.
The folk's own fastness that fiery dragon
with flame had destroyed, and the stronghold all
washed by waves; but the warlike king,
prince of the Weders, plotted vengeance.
Warriors'-bulwark, he bade them work
all of iron—the earl's commander—
a war-shield wondrous: well he knew
that forest-wood against fire were worthless,
linden could aid not.—Atheling brave,
he was fated to finish this fleeting life,

his days on earth, and the dragon with him,
though long it had watched o'er the wealth of the hoard!—
Shame he reckoned it, sharer-of-rings,
to follow the flyer-afar with a host,
a broad-flung band; nor the battle feared he,
nor deemed he dreadful the dragon's warring,
its vigor and valor: ventures desperate
he had passed a-plenty, and perils of war,
contest-crash, since, conqueror proud,
Hrothgar's hall he had wholly purged,
and in grapple had killed the kin of Grendel,
loathsome breed! Not least was that
of hand-to-hand fights where Hygelac fell,
when the ruler of Geats in rush of battle,
lord of his folk, in the Frisian land,
son of Hrethel, by sword-draughts died,
by brands down-beaten. Thence Beowulf fled
through strength of himself and his swimming power,
though alone, and his arms were laden with thirty
coats of mail, when he came to the sea!
Nor yet might Hetwaras haughtily boast
their craft of contest, who carried against him
shields to the fight: but few escaped
from strife with the hero to seek their homes!
Then swam over ocean Ecgtheow's son
lonely and sorrowful, seeking his land,
where Hygd made him offer of hoard and realm,
rings and royal-seat, reckoning naught
the strength of her son to save their kingdom
from hostile hordes, after Hygelac's death.
No sooner for this could the stricken ones
in any wise move that atheling's mind
over young Heardred's head as lord
and ruler of all the realm to be:

yet the hero upheld him with helpful words,
aided in honor, till, older grown,
he wielded the Weder-Geats.—Wandering exiles
sought him o'er seas, the sons of Ohtere,
who had spurned the sway of the Scylfings'-helmet,
the bravest and best that broke the rings,
in Swedish land, of the sea-kings' line,
haughty hero. Hence Heardred's end.
For shelter he gave them, sword-death came,
the blade's fell blow, to bairn of Hygelac;
but the son of Ongentheow sought again
house and home when Heardred fell,
leaving Beowulf lord of Geats
and gift-seat's master.—A good king he!

Chapter 31

THE dragon burned homes throughout the land, terrifying the people. It killed everyone it saw and cut a path of destruction throughout the Geats' land. Every day at dawn it returned to its lair, where it felt safe.

Then the dragon burned down Beowulf's home, the throne room of the Geats. It was a heavy blow to the old man. Beowulf assumed that God was punishing him for something. He dwelled on his sufferings, which he was never known to do. The dragon destroyed the Geats' forts and defenses along the coast, but Beowulf began to plan his revenge. He ordered his blacksmiths to make a mighty shield. He and the dragon were destined to end their lives together. Beowulf thought it would be shameful to go after the dragon with a whole army. He had fought plenty of difficult battles on his own since the time that he killed Grendel and his mother. He had wrestled with monsters and won. One of those battles was the one that took the life of Hygelac, the former king. After that battle was over, Beowulf swam through the sea wearing thirty sets of armor, which was the plunder he took from the war. None of his enemies would dare to face him after that. When he returned from that war, Queen Hygd offered Beowulf the kingdom. She didn't believe her son Heardred could be a good king and keep the Geats safe. But Beowulf couldn't be convinced to take over. Instead, he assisted and advised Heardred until Hygelac's son grew up and was able to protect the Geats. About that time, some exiles from the wars in Sweden came and Heardred gave them shelter. But the Swedes came looking for the exiles, and in the battle Heardred was killed. Onela took the throne in Sweden, leaving Beowulf to become a great king for the Geats. He was a good king.

Chapter 32

THE fall of his lord he was fain to requite
in after days; and to Eadgils he proved
friend to the friendless, and forces sent
over the sea to the son of Ohtere,
weapons and warriors: well repaid he
those care-paths cold when the king he slew.
Thus safe through struggles the son of Ecgtheow
had passed a plenty, through perils dire,
with daring deeds, till this day was come
that doomed him now with the dragon to strive.

With comrades eleven the lord of Geats
swollen in rage went seeking the dragon.
He had heard whence all the harm arose
and the killing of clansmen; that cup of price
on the lap of the lord had been laid by the finder.
In the throng was this one thirteenth man,
starter of all the strife and ill,
care-laden captive; cringing thence
forced and reluctant, he led them on
till he came in ken of that cavern-hall,
the barrow delved near billowy surges,
flood of ocean. Within 'twas full
of wire-gold and jewels; a jealous warden,
warrior trusty, the treasures held,
lurked in his lair. Not light the task
of entrance for any of earth-born men!

Sat on the headland the hero king,
spake words of hail to his hearth-companions,
gold-friend of Geats. All gloomy his soul,
wavering, death-bound. Wyrd full nigh

Beowulf

stood ready to greet the gray-haired man,
to seize his soul-hoard, sunder apart
life and body. Not long would be
the warrior's spirit enwound with flesh.

Beowulf spake, the bairn of Ecgtheow:—
"Through store of struggles I strove in youth,
mighty feuds; I mind them all.
I was seven years old when the sovran of rings,
friend-of-his-folk, from my father took me,
had me, and held me, Hrethel the king,
with food and fee, faithful in kinship.
Ne'er, while I lived there, he loathlier found me,
bairn in the burg, than his birthright sons,
Herebeald and Haethcyn and Hygelac mine.
For the eldest of these, by unmeet chance,
by kinsman's deed, was the death-bed strewn,
when Haethcyn killed him with horny bow,
his own dear liege laid low with an arrow,
missed the mark and his mate shot down,
one brother the other, with bloody shaft.
A feeless fight, and a fearful sin,
horror to Hrethel; yet, hard as it was,
unavenged must the atheling die!
Too awful it is for an aged man
to bide and bear, that his bairn so young
rides on the gallows. A rime he makes,
sorrow-song for his son there hanging
as rapture of ravens; no rescue now
can come from the old, disabled man!
Still is he minded, as morning breaks,
of the heir gone elsewhere; another he hopes not
he will bide to see his burg within
as ward for his wealth, now the one has found

doom of death that the deed incurred.
Forlorn he looks on the lodge of his son,
wine-hall waste and wind-swept chambers
reft of revel. The rider sleepeth,
the hero, far-hidden; no harp resounds,
in the courts no wassail, as once was heard."

Chapter 32

BEOWULF immediately avenged Heardred and ended the feuding in Sweden by killing Onela. Thus he showed his ability to survive dangerous situations time and again, until the day came when fate forced him to battle the dragon.

Beowulf took eleven of his men and went in search of the dragon. They met up with the man who had taken the goblet out of the dragon's lair and Beowulf learned the whole story of how the dragon's rage was awakened. This man joined their war party and led them to the dragon's lair.

Beowulf spoke to his men before leading them in. Fate had brought him to the place of his death, and his speech was dark.

"I have fought many battles, and I remember them all. When I was seven, King Hrethel took responsibility for me from my father. He treated me well, no different from his own sons, Herebeald, Heathcyn, and Hygelac. Heathcyn accidentally killed Herebeald with an arrow, which was a terrible blow to their father. He was unable to avenge his son's death, since his other son had caused it. It was like a man watching his son be executed."

Chapter 33

THEN he goes to his chamber, a grief-song chants
alone for his lost. Too large all seems,
homestead and house. So the helmet-of-Weders
hid in his heart for Herebeald
waves of woe. No way could he take
to avenge on the slayer slaughter so foul;
nor e'en could he harass that hero at all
with loathing deed, though he loved him not.
And so for the sorrow his soul endured,
men's gladness he gave up and God's light chose.
Lands and cities he left his sons
(as the wealthy do) when he went from earth.
There was strife and struggle 'twixt Swede and Geat
o'er the width of waters; war arose,
hard battle-horror, when Hrethel died,
and Ongentheow's offspring grew
strife-keen, bold, nor brooked o'er the seas
pact of peace, but pushed their hosts
to harass in hatred by Hreosnabeorh.
Men of my folk for that feud had vengeance,
for woful war ('tis widely known),
though one of them bought it with blood of his heart,
a bargain hard: for Haethcyn proved
fatal that fray, for the first-of-Geats.
At morn, I heard, was the murderer killed
by kinsman for kinsman, with clash of sword,
when Ongentheow met Eofor there.
Wide split the war-helm: wan he fell,
hoary Scylfing; the hand that smote him
of feud was mindful, nor flinched from the death-blow.

* * *

—For all that he gave me, my gleaming sword
repaid him at war,—such power I wielded,—
for lordly treasure: with land he entrusted me,
homestead and house. He had no need
from Swedish realm, or from Spear-Dane folk,
or from men of the Gifths, to get him help,—
some warrior worse for wage to buy!
Ever I fought in the front of all,
sole to the fore; and so shall I fight
while I bide in life and this blade shall last
that early and late hath loyal proved
since for my doughtiness Daeghrefn fell,
slain by my hand, the Hugas' champion.
Nor fared he thence to the Frisian king
with the booty back, and breast-adornments;
but, slain in struggle, that standard-bearer
fell, atheling brave. Not with blade was he slain,
but his bones were broken by brawny gripe,
his heart-waves stilled.—The sword-edge now,
hard blade and my hand, for the hoard shall strive."

Beowulf spake, and a battle-vow made
his last of all: "I have lived through many
wars in my youth; now once again,
old folk-defender, feud will I seek,
do doughty deeds, if the dark destroyer
forth from his cavern come to fight me!"
Then hailed he the helmeted heroes all,
for the last time greeting his liegemen dear,
comrades of war: "I should carry no weapon,
no sword to the serpent, if sure I knew
how, with such enemy, else my vows
I could gain as I did in Grendel's day.
But fire in this fight I must fear me now,

and poisonous breath; so I bring with me
breastplate and board. From the barrow's keeper
no footbreadth flee I. One fight shall end
our war by the wall, as Wyrd allots,
all mankind's master. My mood is bold
but forbears to boast o'er this battling-flyer.
—Now abide by the barrow, ye breastplate-mailed,
ye heroes in harness, which of us twain
better from battle-rush bear his wounds.
Wait ye the finish. The fight is not yours,
nor meet for any but me alone
to measure might with this monster here
and play the hero. Hardily I
shall win that wealth, or war shall seize,
cruel killing, your king and lord!"

Up stood then with shield the sturdy champion,
stayed by the strength of his single manhood,
and hardy 'neath helmet his harness bore
under cleft of the cliffs: no coward's path!
Soon spied by the wall that warrior chief,
survivor of many a victory-field
where foemen fought with furious clashings,
an arch of stone; and within, a stream
that broke from the barrow. The brooklet's wave
was hot with fire. The hoard that way
he never could hope unharmed to near,
or endure those deeps, for the dragon's flame.
Then let from his breast, for he burst with rage,
the Weder-Geat prince a word outgo;
stormed the stark-heart; stern went ringing
and clear his cry 'neath the cliff-rocks gray.
The hoard-guard heard a human voice;
his rage was enkindled. No respite now

for pact of peace! The poison-breath
of that foul worm first came forth from the cave,
hot reek-of-fight: the rocks resounded.
Stout by the stone-way his shield he raised,
lord of the Geats, against the loathed-one;
while with courage keen that coiled foe
came seeking strife. The sturdy king
had drawn his sword, not dull of edge,
heirloom old; and each of the two
felt fear of his foe, though fierce their mood.
Stoutly stood with his shield high-raised
the warrior king, as the worm now coiled
together amain: the mailed-one waited.
Now, spire by spire, fast sped and glided
that blazing serpent. The shield protected,
soul and body a shorter while
for the hero-king than his heart desired,
could his will have wielded the welcome respite
but once in his life! But Wyrd denied it,
and victory's honors.—His arm he lifted
lord of the Geats, the grim foe smote
with atheling's heirloom. Its edge was turned
brown blade, on the bone, and bit more feebly
than its noble master had need of then
in his baleful stress.—Then the barrow's keeper
waxed full wild for that weighty blow,
cast deadly flames; wide drove and far
those vicious fires. No victor's glory
the Geats' lord boasted; his brand had failed,
naked in battle, as never it should,
excellent iron!—'Twas no easy path
that Ecgtheow's honored heir must tread
over the plain to the place of the foe;
for against his will he must win a home

elsewhere far, as must all men, leaving
this lapsing life!—Not long it was
ere those champions grimly closed again.
The hoard-guard was heartened; high heaved his breast
once more; and by peril was pressed again,
enfolded in flames, the folk-commander!
Nor yet about him his band of comrades,
sons of athelings, armed stood
with warlike front: to the woods they bent them,
their lives to save. But the soul of one
with care was cumbered. Kinship true
can never be marred in a noble mind!

Chapter 33

HRETHEL lost his mind," Beowulf continued. "He was unable to enjoy anything after that, knowing that his firstborn son was lying in the ground and that he could not take revenge on the killer. He eventually faded away into death. After Hrethel died, there were many wars between the Swedes and the Geats. My own family fought bravely in these battles, as everyone knows. Haethcyn was killed in one of these combats, and Hygelac went to war against his brother's killer. Eofor, one of Hygelac's men, killed the Swedish king Ongentheow.

"I fought bravely with Hygelac and was rewarded with treasure and land. He didn't have to look anywhere else for help or hire any mercenaries. I always fought in the front, and I always will. I killed mighty warriors with my bare hands. Now I will battle this dragon with those same hands and my sword."

Beowulf made one last battle vow. "I have survived many wars, and I will fight one more now if the dragon dares to face me. I would rather not carry a weapon, but his fire and poisonous breath are powerful, so I will keep my armor and my shield. I will stand my ground when I face him and God will decide the victor. Stay out here, men. Wait to see who emerges from the struggle. This is no one's fight but mine. Either I will earn glory and wealth, or you will lose your king."

Beowulf rose and climbed up the face of the cliff toward the dragon's lair. He did not try to sneak in like a coward. He soon saw a stone arch with a stream of fire leading out of it. It would be dangerous to enter that way because of the flames. He cried out with rage, a shout that woke the dragon within. Any chance at peace was over now. The dragon's poisonous breath came pouring out of the lair. Beowulf raised his shield and his sword. Both he and the dragon were ferocious, but each was afraid of the other. Beowulf stood his ground as the dragon charged. His shield was not as strong as he wished. That was the first time he had battled that fate had denied him glory. Beowulf swung his sword. The dragon screamed beneath the king's blow, but the blade was not as strong as Beowulf had hoped. The sword had not cut through the dragon. For the first time, it had failed. Beowulf had to give up his ground and move, just as all men must give up their lives. They clashed again. The dragon boldly struck out at the king and surrounded him in flame. Beowulf's men had retreated to the woods to save their lives. Only one man remained to fight with Beowulf, a man whose feeling of kinship came through strongly, as it always does in noble men.

Chapter 34

WIGLAF his name was, Weohstan's son,
linden-thane loved, the lord of Scylfings,
Aelfhere's kinsman. His king he now saw
with heat under helmet hard oppressed.
He minded the prizes his prince had given him,
wealthy seat of the Waegmunding line,
and folk-rights that his father owned
Not long he lingered. The linden yellow,
his shield, he seized; the old sword he drew:—
as heirloom of Eanmund earth-dwellers knew it,
who was slain by the sword-edge, son of Ohtere,
friendless exile, erst in fray
killed by Weohstan, who won for his kin
brown-bright helmet, breastplate ringed,
old sword of Eotens, Onela's gift,
weeds of war of the warrior-thane,
battle-gear brave: though a brother's child
had been felled, the feud was unfelt by Onela.
For winters this war-gear Weohstan kept,
breastplate and board, till his bairn had grown
earlship to earn as the old sire did:
then he gave him, mid Geats, the gear of battle,
portion huge, when he passed from life,
fared aged forth. For the first time now
with his leader-lord the liegeman young
was bidden to share the shock of battle.
Neither softened his soul, nor the sire's bequest
weakened in war. So the worm found out
when once in fight the foes had met!
Wiglaf spake,—and his words were sage;
sad in spirit, he said to his comrades:—
"I remember the time, when mead we took,
what promise we made to this prince of ours

Beowulf

in the banquet-hall, to our breaker-of-rings,
for gear of combat to give him requital,
for hard-sword and helmet, if hap should bring
stress of this sort! Himself who chose us
from all his army to aid him now,
urged us to glory, and gave these treasures,
because he counted us keen with the spear
and hardy 'neath helm, though this hero-work
our leader hoped unhelped and alone
to finish for us,—folk-defender
who hath got him glory greater than all men
for daring deeds! Now the day is come
that our noble master has need of the might
of warriors stout. Let us stride along
the hero to help while the heat is about him
glowing and grim! For God is my witness
I am far more fain the fire should seize
along with my lord these limbs of mine!
Unsuiting it seems our shields to bear
homeward hence, save here we essay
to fell the foe and defend the life
of the Weders' lord. I wot 'twere shame
on the law of our land if alone the king
out of Geatish warriors woe endured
and sank in the struggle! My sword and helmet,
breastplate and board, for us both shall serve!"
Through slaughter-reek strode he to succor his chieftain,
his battle-helm bore, and brief words spake:—
"Beowulf dearest, do all bravely,
as in youthful days of yore thou vowedst
that while life should last thou wouldst let no wise
thy glory droop! Now, great in deeds,
atheling steadfast, with all thy strength
shield thy life! I will stand to help thee."

* * *

Beowulf

At the words the worm came once again,
murderous monster mad with rage,
with fire-billows flaming, its foes to seek,
the hated men. In heat-waves burned
that board to the boss, and the breastplate failed
to shelter at all the spear-thane young.
Yet quickly under his kinsman's shield
went eager the earl, since his own was now
all burned by the blaze. The bold king again
had mind of his glory: with might his glaive
was driven into the dragon's head,—
blow nerved by hate. But Naegling was shivered,
broken in battle was Beowulf's sword,
old and gray. 'Twas granted him not
that ever the edge of iron at all
could help him at strife: too strong was his hand,
so the tale is told, and he tried too far
with strength of stroke all swords he wielded,
though sturdy their steel: they steaded him nought.
Then for the third time thought on its feud
that folk-destroyer, fire-dread dragon,
and rushed on the hero, where room allowed,
battle-grim, burning; its bitter teeth
closed on his neck, and covered him
with waves of blood from his breast that welled.

Chapter 34

THAT man's name was Wiglaf. He saw that Beowulf was surrounded by flames, and he remembered all of the good things his king had done for him. Wiglaf carried an ancient sword, supposedly inherited from ancient Eanmund. The sword was given to Wiglaf's father, Weohstan, after he slayed the son of Ohtere in the battle with the Swedes. Wiglaf charged into battle, and that great sword did not break, as the dragon soon discovered. Wiglaf called out to his comrades. "I remember when we were in the mead hall and we promised to bring Beowulf swords and armor if he needed them. He picked us to join him out of all his soldiers because he believed we were good with our swords. Though he told us to let him fight the dragon himself, he needs us now. Let's help him! With God as my witness, I'd rather die in the fire than go back home still carrying my weapons. It would be a terrible shame if we let our king die and we all survived. My sword and armor will be enough for both of us." Wiglaf approached Beowulf and said, "Be brave, dear Beowulf, as you were in your youth. Defend yourself, great warrior! I will stand by your side."

The dragon heard Wiglaf and came roaring forward, its breath flaming. Wiglaf's shield burned away and his armor was almost useless, but he managed to get behind Beowulf's shield. Beowulf was spurred to action by the thoughts of glory that Wiglaf had inspired. He swung the sword with all his might and drove it into the dragon's head. The sword shattered. It is said that Beowulf could not use swords in battle, because he was too strong and broke them all. The dragon lunged forward and bit Beowulf on the neck, sending blood pouring forth.

Chapter 35

T WAS now, men say, in his sovran's need
   that the earl made known his noble strain,
craft and keenness and courage enduring.
Heedless of harm, though his hand was burned,
hardy-hearted, he helped his kinsman.
A little lower the loathsome beast
he smote with sword; his steel drove in
bright and burnished; that blaze began
to lose and lessen. At last the king
wielded his wits again, war-knife drew,
a biting blade by his breastplate hanging,
and the Weders'-helm smote that worm asunder,
felled the foe, flung forth its life.

So had they killed it, kinsmen both,
athelings twain: thus an earl should be
in danger's day!—Of deeds of valor
this conqueror's-hour of the king was last,
of his work in the world. The wound began,
which that dragon-of-earth had erst inflicted,
to swell and smart; and soon he found
in his breast was boiling, baleful and deep,
pain of poison. The prince walked on,
wise in his thought, to the wall of rock;
then sat, and stared at the structure of giants,
where arch of stone and steadfast column
upheld forever that hall in earth.
Yet here must the hand of the henchman peerless
lave with water his winsome lord,
the king and conqueror covered with blood,
with struggle spent, and unspan his helmet.
Beowulf spake in spite of his hurt,

his mortal wound; full well he knew
his portion now was past and gone
of earthly bliss, and all had fled
of his file of days, and death was near:
"I would fain bestow on son of mine
this gear of war, were given me now
that any heir should after me come
of my proper blood. This people I ruled
fifty winters. No folk-king was there,
none at all, of the neighboring clans
who war would wage me with 'warriors'-friends'
and threat me with horrors. At home I bided
what fate might come, and I cared for mine own;
feuds I sought not, nor falsely swore
ever on oath. For all these things,
though fatally wounded, fain am I!
From the Ruler-of-Man no wrath shall seize me,
when life from my frame must flee away,
for killing of kinsmen! Now quickly go
and gaze on that hoard 'neath the hoary rock,
Wiglaf loved, now the worm lies low,
sleeps, heart-sore, of his spoil bereaved.
And fare in haste. I would fain behold
the gorgeous heirlooms, golden store,
have joy in the jewels and gems, lay down
softlier for sight of this splendid hoard
my life and the lordship I long have held."

Chapter 35

I T was at this moment that Wiglaf's bravery revealed itself. Even though his hand was badly burned, he drove his blade into the dragon's stomach. Its fiery breath weakened. Beowulf regained his strength. He pulled his knife out and stabbed at the dragon's side. The blow was fatal.

Together, the two brave men had killed the beast. This was the last act of glory the king would ever perform. The dragon's poison ran through his blood. He walked out of the lair and sat at the edge of the cliff. Beowulf looked up at the cliff face. The giant stones had held up the earth for ages. Wiglaf approached and washed his king's wound. Beowulf knew that his life was ending. Despite his wound, he spoke to the loyal Wiglaf. "I would have liked to have given my armor to my son, if only fate had given me one. I have ruled the Geats for fifty years. No other king would dare challenge me. I focused on our own affairs and did not seek out wars or troubles, and I never broke a promise. Even though I am dying, the thought of all of this is a comfort. I never killed my kinsmen and have nothing to fear from the Ruler of Mankind. Go and look at the treasure while the dragon is dying, dear Wiglaf. I want to see those beautiful jewels before I die. It will make my death easier to see all that treasure and think of my long rule."

Chapter 36

I HAVE heard that swiftly the son of Weohstan
at wish and word of his wounded king,—
war-sick warrior,—woven mail-coat,
battle-sark, bore 'neath the barrow's roof.
Then the clansman keen, of conquest proud,
passing the seat, saw store of jewels
and glistening gold the ground along;
by the wall were marvels, and many a vessel
in the den of the dragon, the dawn-flier old:
unburnished bowls of bygone men
reft of richness; rusty helms
of the olden age; and arm-rings many
wondrously woven.—Such wealth of gold,
booty from barrow, can burden with pride
each human wight: let him hide it who will!—
His glance too fell on a gold-wove banner
high o'er the hoard, of handiwork noblest,
brilliantly broidered; so bright its gleam,
all the earth-floor he easily saw
and viewed all these vessels. No vestige now
was seen of the serpent: the sword had ta'en him.

Then, I heard, the hill of its hoard was reft,
old work of giants, by one alone;
he burdened his bosom with beakers and plate
at his own good will, and the ensign took,
brightest of beacons.—The blade of his lord
—its edge was iron—had injured deep
one that guarded the golden hoard
many a year and its murder-fire
spread hot round the barrow in horror-billows
at midnight hour, till it met its doom.

Hasted the herald, the hoard so spurred him
his track to retrace; he was troubled by doubt,
high-souled hero, if haply he'd find
alive, where he left him, the lord of Weders,
weakening fast by the wall of the cave.
So he carried the load. His lord and king
he found all bleeding, famous chief
at the lapse of life. The liegeman again
plashed him with water, till point of word
broke through the breast-hoard. Beowulf spake,
sage and sad, as he stared at the gold.—
"For the gold and treasure, to God my thanks,
to the Wielder-of-Wonders, with words I say,
for what I behold, to Heaven's Lord,
for the grace that I give such gifts to my folk
or ever the day of my death be run!
Now I've bartered here for booty of treasure
the last of my life, so look ye well
to the needs of my land! No longer I tarry.
A barrow bid ye the battle-fanned raise
for my ashes. 'Twill shine by the shore of the flood,
to folk of mine memorial fair
on Hrones Headland high uplifted,
that ocean-wanderers oft may hail
Beowulf's Barrow, as back from far
they drive their keels o'er the darkling wave."

From his neck he unclasped the collar of gold,
valorous king, to his vassal gave it
with bright-gold helmet, breastplate, and ring,
to the youthful thane: bade him use them in joy.

"Thou art end and remnant of all our race
the Waegmunding name. For Wyrd hath swept them,

all my line, to the land of doom,
earls in their glory: I after them go."
This word was the last which the wise old man
harbored in heart ere hot death-waves
of balefire he chose. From his bosom fled
his soul to seek the saints' reward.

Chapter 36

WIGLAF went into the lair. He saw jewels and gold shining everywhere. There were ancient goblets and helmets, as well as beautiful jewelry of all kinds. Any man can lose great treasure, no matter how well he hides it. Wiglaf saw a beautiful banner hanging on one wall. It was so bright that it allowed him to see all around inside the lair. The dragon was dead.

Wiglaf filled his arms with treasure and ran back out to Beowulf, hoping that his king would be alive. Beowulf was bleeding to death. Wiglaf splashed him with water to revive him. "I thank God for being able to see such treasure," Beowulf said, "and for being able to give it to my people when I die. I've traded my life for this treasure. Look after the needs of my people. I will not be here much longer. After my funeral pyre has burned, build a mound in my name so that people will pass under it and remember me. They will call it Beowulf's Barrow."

Beowulf removed his necklace, helmet, breastplate, and ring, and gave them to Wiglaf.

"You are the last of the Waegmunding family. Fate has taken all of my line to the land of doom, and now I join them." Those were the last words he said. His soul left his body to seek its reward.

Chapter 37

I T was heavy hap for that hero young
on his lord beloved to look and find him
lying on earth with life at end,
sorrowful sight. But the slayer too,
awful earth-dragon, empty of breath,
lay felled in fight, nor, fain of its treasure,
could the writhing monster rule it more.
For edges of iron had ended its days,
hard and battle-sharp, hammers' leaving;
and that flier-afar had fallen to ground
hushed by its hurt, its hoard all near,
no longer lusty aloft to whirl
at midnight, making its merriment seen,
proud of its prizes: prone it sank
by the handiwork of the hero-king.
Forsooth among folk but few achieve,
—though sturdy and strong, as stories tell me,
and never so daring in deed of valor,—
the perilous breath of a poison-foe
to brave, and to rush on the ring-board hall,
whenever his watch the warden keeps
bold in the barrow. Beowulf paid
the price of death for that precious hoard;
and each of the foes had found the end
of this fleeting life.

Befell erelong
that the laggards in war the wood had left,
trothbreakers, cowards, ten together,
fearing before to flourish a spear
in the sore distress of their sovran lord.
Now in their shame their shields they carried,

armor of fight, where the old man lay;
and they gazed on Wiglaf. Wearied he sat
at his sovran's shoulder, shieldsman good,
to wake him with water. Nowise it availed.
Though well he wished it, in world no more
could he barrier life for that leader-of-battles
nor baffle the will of all-wielding God.
Doom of the Lord was law o'er the deeds
of every man, as it is to-day.
Grim was the answer, easy to get,
from the youth for those that had yielded to fear!
Wiglaf spake, the son of Weohstan,—
mournful he looked on those men unloved:—
"Who sooth will speak, can say indeed
that the ruler who gave you golden rings
and the harness of war in which ye stand
—for he at ale-bench often-times
bestowed on hall-folk helm and breastplate,
lord to liegemen, the likeliest gear
which near of far he could find to give,—
threw away and wasted these weeds of battle,
on men who failed when the foemen came!
Not at all could the king of his comrades-in-arms
venture to vaunt, though the Victory-Wielder,
God, gave him grace that he got revenge
sole with his sword in stress and need.
To rescue his life, 'twas little that I
could serve him in struggle; yet shift I made
(hopeless it seemed) to help my kinsman.
Its strength ever waned, when with weapon I struck
that fatal foe, and the fire less strongly
flowed from its head.—Too few the heroes
in throe of contest that thronged to our king!
Now gift of treasure and girding of sword,

joy of the house and home-delight
shall fail your folk; his freehold-land
every clansman within your kin
shall lose and leave, when lords highborn
hear afar of that flight of yours,
a fameless deed. Yea, death is better
for liegemen all than a life of shame!"

Chapter 37

I T was difficult for Wiglaf to watch Beowulf die. But his killer was dead as well. Blades had ended its life and made sure that it wouldn't haunt the land at night any longer. There are few men, even among the bravest, who would dare face a dragon's fire and poison breath. Beowulf paid for the dragon's treasure with his life, but he killed every enemy he ever fought.

The other men approached. They had been too afraid to come to Beowulf's aid, and now they were ashamed. They saw Wiglaf sitting beside their dead king, trying to revive Beowulf. It was too late. He could not bring that great warrior back from where God had taken him. The Lord's will rules over every man. The cowardly men looked at Wiglaf's grim face. He looked up at them and said, "Anyone can see that all of the gifts Beowulf gave you were a waste. You threw away the honor he showed you when you refused to help him. Our king had no reason to brag about his men. God favored him by helping him to kill that dragon with his own sword. There wasn't much I could do to help him, but I did the little that I could. I weakened the dragon by stabbing it with my sword. It's a shame that I was the only one to help. Now all of this treasure will be useless to you. Men will lose their feelings of loyalty to you, and your lands will become deserted. It's better for a warrior to die than to live a life of shame."

Chapter 38

THAT battle-toil bade he at burg to announce,
at the fort on the cliff, where, full of sorrow,
all the morning earls had sat,
daring shieldsmen, in doubt of twain:
would they wail as dead, or welcome home,
their lord beloved? Little kept back
of the tidings new, but told them all,
the herald that up the headland rode.—
"Now the willing-giver to Weder folk
in death-bed lies; the Lord of Geats
on the slaughter-bed sleeps by the serpent's deed!
And beside him is stretched that slayer-of-men
with knife-wounds sick: no sword availed
on the awesome thing in any wise
to work a wound. There Wiglaf sitteth,
Weohstan's bairn, by Beowulf's side,
the living earl by the other dead,
and heavy of heart a head-watch keeps
o'er friend and foe.—Now our folk may look
for waging of war when once unhidden
to Frisian and Frank the fall of the king
is spread afar.—The strife began
when hot on the Hugas Hygelac fell
and fared with his fleet to the Frisian land.
Him there the Hetwaras humbled in war,
plied with such prowess their power o'erwhelming
that the bold-in-battle bowed beneath it
and fell in fight. To his friends no wise
could that earl give treasure! And ever since
the Merowings' favor has failed us wholly.
Nor aught expect I of peace and faith
from Swedish folk. 'Twas spread afar

Beowulf

how Ongentheow reft at Ravenswood
Haethcyn Hrethling of hope and life,
when the folk of Geats for the first time sought
in wanton pride the Warlike-Scylfings.
Soon the sage old sire of Ohtere,
ancient and awful, gave answering blow;
the sea-king he slew, and his spouse redeemed,
his good wife rescued, though robbed of her gold,
mother of Ohtere and Onela.
Then he followed his foes, who fled before him
sore beset and stole their way,
bereft of a ruler, to Ravenswood.

"With his host he besieged there what swords had left,
the weary and wounded; woes he threatened
the whole night through to that hard-pressed throng:
some with the morrow his sword should kill,
some should go to the gallows-tree
for rapture of ravens. But rescue came
with dawn of day for those desperate men
when they heard the horn of Hygelac sound,
tones of his trumpet; the trusty king
had followed their trail with faithful band."

Chapter 38

W IGLAF ordered that news of the battle be spread to the men who had camped nearby, so they wouldn't be left wondering what had happened. The messenger told everything. "The king of the Geats is dead. His body rests beside that of the dragon he killed. Wiglaf sits beside Beowulf's body with a heavy heart. Our people can expect war to come now that our great protector is dead. The same thing happened when Hygelac was killed. The Franks, Frisians, and Swedes will all likely come for a fight. The Franks have been eager to fight us ever since Hygelac invaded Friesland. There the Frankish tribe of Hetware killed him and defeated his army. The Franks have been the Geats' enemy ever since. We should not expect the Swedes to honor their promises of peace either. Remember that the Geats attacked them out of arrogance and kidnapped their queen. The Swedes struck back. King Ongentheow rescued his wife and killed Haethcyn, who was Hrethel's son and king of the Geats. Ongentheow routed the Geats at Ravenswood.

"Ongentheow's men surrounded the Geats and taunted them, vowing to feed their bodies to the birds. But as dawn broke, Hygelac and his men arrived to save their kinsmen."

Chapter 39

THE bloody swath of Swedes and Geats
    and the storm of their strife, were seen afar,
how folk against folk the fight had wakened.
The ancient king with his atheling band
sought his citadel, sorrowing much:
Ongentheow earl went up to his burg.
He had tested Hygelac's hardihood,
the proud one's prowess, would prove it no longer,
defied no more those fighting-wanderers
nor hoped from the seamen to save his hoard,
his bairn and his bride: so he bent him again,
old, to his earth-walls. Yet after him came
with slaughter for Swedes the standards of Hygelac
o'er peaceful plains in pride advancing,
till Hrethelings fought in the fenced town.
Then Ongentheow with edge of sword,
the hoary-bearded, was held at bay,
and the folk-king there was forced to suffer
Eofor's anger. In ire, at the king
Wulf Wonreding with weapon struck;
and the chieftain's blood, for that blow, in streams
flowed 'neath his hair. No fear felt he,
stout old Scylfing, but straightway repaid
in better bargain that bitter stroke
and faced his foe with fell intent.
Nor swift enough was the son of Wonred
answer to render the aged chief;
too soon on his head the helm was cloven;
blood-bedecked he bowed to earth,
and fell adown; not doomed was he yet,
and well he waxed, though the wound was sore.
Then the hardy Hygelac-thane,

Beowulf

when his brother fell, with broad brand smote,
giants' sword crashing through giants'-helm
across the shield-wall: sank the king,
his folk's old herdsman, fatally hurt.
There were many to bind the brother's wounds
and lift him, fast as fate allowed
his people to wield the place-of-war.
But Eofor took from Ongentheow,
earl from other, the iron-breastplate,
hard sword hilted, and helmet too,
and the hoar-chief's harness to Hygelac carried,
who took the trappings, and truly promised
rich fee 'mid folk,—and fulfilled it so.
For that grim strife gave the Geatish lord,
Hrethel's offspring, when home he came,
to Eofor and Wulf a wealth of treasure,
Each of them had a hundred thousand
in land and linked rings; nor at less price reckoned
mid-earth men such mighty deeds!
And to Eofor he gave his only daughter
in pledge of grace, the pride of his home."

"Such is the feud, the foeman's rage,
death-hate of men: so I deem it sure
that the Swedish folk will seek us home
for this fall of their friends, the fighting-Scylfings,
when once they learn that our warrior leader
lifeless lies, who land and hoard
ever defended from all his foes,
furthered his folk's weal, finished his course
a hardy hero.—Now haste is best,
that we go to gaze on our Geatish lord,
and bear the bountiful breaker-of-rings
to the funeral pyre. No fragments merely

Beowulf

shall burn with the warrior. Wealth of jewels,
gold untold and gained in terror,
treasure at last with his life obtained,
all of that booty the brands shall take,
fire shall eat it. No earl must carry
memorial jewel. No maiden fair
shall wreathe her neck with noble ring:
nay, sad in spirit and shorn of her gold,
oft shall she pass o'er paths of exile
now our lord all laughter has laid aside,
all mirth and revel. Many a spear
morning-cold shall be clasped amain,
lifted aloft; nor shall lilt of harp
those warriors wake; but the wan-hued raven,
fain o'er the fallen, his feast shall praise
and boast to the eagle how bravely he ate
when he and the wolf were wasting the slain."

So he told his sorrowful tidings,
and little he lied, the loyal man
of word or of work. The warriors rose;
sad, they climbed to the Cliff-of-Eagles,
went, welling with tears, the wonder to view.
Found on the sand there, stretched at rest,
their lifeless lord, who had lavished rings
of old upon them. Ending-day
had dawned on the doughty-one; death had seized
in woful slaughter the Weders' king.
There saw they, besides, the strangest being,
loathsome, lying their leader near,
prone on the field. The fiery dragon,
fearful fiend, with flame was scorched.
Reckoned by feet, it was fifty measures
in length as it lay. Aloft erewhile

Beowulf

it had revelled by night, and anon come back,
seeking its den; now in death's sure clutch
it had come to the end of its earth-hall joys.
By it there stood the stoups and jars;
dishes lay there, and dear-decked swords
eaten with rust, as, on earth's lap resting,
a thousand winters they waited there.
For all that heritage huge, that gold
of bygone men, was bound by a spell,
so the treasure-hall could be touched by none
of human kind,—save that Heaven's King,
God himself, might give whom he would,
Helper of Heroes, the hoard to open,—
even such a man as seemed to him meet.

Chapter 39

THE blood from the battles between the Geats and the Swedes ran throughout the land," Wiglaf continued. "Everyone saw it. Eventually Ongentheow and his men retreated to high ground. Ongentheow knew what a great warrior Hygelac was and that he could not outlast the mighty Geats. Hygelac led his men into battle, preparing to deliver the final blow. Geatish soldiers soon surrounded Ongentheow. Two brothers, Eofor and Wulf, came at him. Wulf cracked the king's head open, causing blood to run under his hair. But the Swedish king returned the blow and blocked Wulf's sword. So Eofor attacked, breaking through Ongentheow's shield and helmet and killing him. The Geats took Ongentheow's armor and gave it to their leader. Hygelac promised them a great reward, and when they returned home, he delivered. He even gave Eofor his only daughter.

"Now the Swedes will seek revenge for the death of Ongentheow. They will come to our lands and attack us, I imagine. Beowulf kept us safe, but now he is gone. Now, let us go back to look at Beowulf's body one last time and carry him to the funeral pyre. We will burn all of the treasure with it. No one should carry any of those jewels as relics or memorials. No maiden will wear these jewels around her neck. No harp will sound to lift our spirits. But the raven will fly to the eagle and tell of how he saw the dead bodies and how he and the wolf made short work of the corpses."

The warriors heard this sad news and went to the cliff to see the horrible sight. They saw their leader's body stretched out, cold and dead. Near it, they saw the horrible dragon, which they measured at fifty feet. It had soared through the night once, but its journeys were over now. Next to the dragon's body was a pile of old and decaying plates, cups, and swords. The golden treasure was under a spell that prevented any man from entering the innermost part of the dragon's lair.

Chapter 40

A PERILOUS path, it proved, he trod
who heinously hid, that hall within,
wealth under wall! Its watcher had killed
one of a few, and the feud was avenged
in woful fashion. Wondrous seems it,
what manner a man of might and valor
oft ends his life, when the earl no longer
in mead-hall may live with loving friends.
So Beowulf, when that barrow's warden
he sought, and the struggle; himself knew not
in what wise he should wend from the world at last.
For princes potent, who placed the gold,
with a curse to doomsday covered it deep,
so that marked with sin the man should be,
hedged with horrors, in hell-bonds fast,
racked with plagues, who should rob their hoard.
Yet no greed for gold, but the grace of heaven,
ever the king had kept in view.

Wiglaf spake, the son of Weohstan:—
"At the mandate of one, oft warriors many
sorrow must suffer; and so must we.
The people's-shepherd showed not aught
of care for our counsel, king beloved!
That guardian of gold he should grapple not, urged we,
but let him lie where he long had been
in his earth-hall waiting the end of the world,
the hest of heaven.—This hoard is ours
but grievously gotten; too grim the fate
which thither carried our king and lord.
I was within there, and all I viewed,
the chambered treasure, when chance allowed me

Beowulf

(and my path was made in no pleasant wise)
under the earth-wall. Eager, I seized
such heap from the hoard as hands could bear
and hurriedly carried it hither back
to my liege and lord. Alive was he still,
still wielding his wits. The wise old man
spake much in his sorrow, and sent you greetings
and bade that ye build, when he breathed no more,
on the place of his balefire a barrow high,
memorial mighty. Of men was he
worthiest warrior wide earth o'er
the while he had joy of his jewels and burg.
Let us set out in haste now, the second time
to see and search this store of treasure,
these wall-hid wonders,—the way I show you,—
where, gathered near, ye may gaze your fill
at broad-gold and rings. Let the bier, soon made,
be all in order when out we come,
our king and captain to carry thither
—man beloved—where long he shall bide
safe in the shelter of sovran God."

Then the bairn of Weohstan bade command,
hardy chief, to heroes many
that owned their homesteads, hither to bring
firewood from far—o'er the folk they ruled—
for the famed-one's funeral. "Fire shall devour
and wan flames feed on the fearless warrior
who oft stood stout in the iron-shower,
when, sped from the string, a storm of arrows
shot o'er the shield-wall: the shaft held firm,
featly feathered, followed the barb."
And now the sage young son of Weohstan
seven chose of the chieftain's thanes,

the best he found that band within,
and went with these warriors, one of eight,
under hostile roof. In hand one bore
a lighted torch and led the way.
No lots they cast for keeping the hoard
when once the warriors saw it in hall,
altogether without a guardian,
lying there lost. And little they mourned
when they had hastily haled it out,
dear-bought treasure! The dragon they cast,
the worm, o'er the wall for the wave to take,
and surges swallowed that shepherd of gems.
Then the woven gold on a wain was laden—
countless quite!—and the king was borne,
hoary hero, to Hrones-Ness.

Chapter 40

THE man who hid his treasure there made a bad decision. The dragon killed him, and it took many deaths before the feud was settled. Even the mightiest man does not know how his life will end. That was the case for Beowulf. He did not know whether his battle with the dragon would be his last. The treasure had been cursed so that those who tried to steal it would suffer, but Beowulf did not look at it with greedy eyes. He wanted it only for his people.

Wiglaf spoke. "One man's decisions can bring suffering to many. That has happened to us here. Our king did not take our advice not to fight the dragon alone. He died for it and earned this treasure, but we cannot enjoy it because of the sad way it came to us. I went into the den and brought back all the treasure I could carry to Beowulf. He was still alive then. He asked that you build a memorial mound for him. He deserves such a mound because he was the mightiest warrior of all. I will take you into the lair so that you can see this amazing treasure. And let's build the pyre so that we can send our beloved king to God."

Wiglaf ordered that wood be brought from the nearby homes in preparation for Beowulf's funeral. "Fire will carry away our brave lord, who stood his ground amidst the flying arrows until one finally hit home." He took the seven best men that were left and went into the dragon's den. He carried a torch to light their way. The men did not fight about who got to take the treasure, as there was so much of it lying there unguarded. They carried it out easily. The men pushed the dragon's body off the cliff and into the sea, where it sank in the waves. Then they carried the treasure and their king to Hrones-Ness.

Chapter 41

THEN fashioned for him the folk of Geats
firm on the earth a funeral-pile,
and hung it with helmets and harness of war
and breastplates bright, as the boon he asked;
and they laid amid it the mighty chieftain,
heroes mourning their master dear.
Then on the hill that hugest of balefires
the warriors wakened. Wood-smoke rose
black over blaze, and blent was the roar
of flame with weeping (the wind was still),
till the fire had broken the frame of bones,
hot at the heart. In heavy mood
their misery moaned they, their master's death.
Wailing her woe, the widow old,
her hair upbound, for Beowulf's death
sung in her sorrow, and said full oft
she dreaded the doleful days to come,
deaths enow, and doom of battle,
and shame.—The smoke by the sky was devoured.

The folk of the Weders fashioned there
on the headland a barrow broad and high,
by ocean-farers far descried:
in ten days' time their toil had raised it,
the battle-brave's beacon. Round brands of the pyre
a wall they built, the worthiest ever
that wit could prompt in their wisest men.
They placed in the barrow that precious booty,
the rounds and the rings they had reft erewhile,
hardy heroes, from hoard in cave,—
trusting the ground with treasure of earls,
gold in the earth, where ever it lies

useless to men as of yore it was.
Then about that barrow the battle-keen rode,
atheling-born, a band of twelve,
lament to make, to mourn their king,
chant their dirge, and their chieftain honor.
They praised his earlship, his acts of prowess
worthily witnessed: and well it is
that men their master-friend mightily laud,
heartily love, when hence he goes
from life in the body forlorn away.

Thus made their mourning the men of Geatland,
for their hero's passing his hearth-companions:
quoth that of all the kings of earth,
of men he was mildest and most beloved,
to his kin the kindest, keenest for praise.

●

Chapter 41

THEY built a large funeral pyre and covered it with armor, just as Beowulf had asked. With heavy hearts, they laid their leader on top. The sound of the crackling fire mixed with the cries of the people gathered there. Beowulf's body collapsed into the flames. An old widow stood nearby, wailing. She mourned her lord and warned of the evil days to come.

As the smoke disappeared into the sky, they started building a mound of earth. It took them ten days to complete it. They surrounded it with a wall and buried the treasure within the mound. Twelve knights rode around the memorial mound. They sang the praises of their departed lord and told of his bravery. It is good for men to praise their masters when they leave this earth.

And this is how the men of Geatland mourned the passing of their king, who was the most eager for glory, the most heroic, the most generous, and the most loving of all the kings of earth.